Hell Squad: Gabe

Anna Hackett

Gabe

Published by Anna Hackett
Copyright 2015 by Anna Hackett
Cover by Melody Simmons of eBookindiecovers
Edits by Tanya Saari

ISBN (eBook): 978-0-9941948-5-5
ISBN (paperback): 978-0-9941948-9-3

What readers are saying about Anna's Science Fiction Romance

At Star's End - One of Library Journal's Best E-Original Romances for 2014

The Phoenix Adventures — SFR Galaxy Award winner for Most Fun New Series

The Anomaly Series — An Action Adventure Romance Bestseller

"Action, danger, aliens, romance – yup, it's another great book from Anna Hackett!" – Book Gannet Reviews, review of *Hell Squad: Marcus*

"Action, adventure, heartache and hot steamy love scenes." – Amazon reviewer, review of *Hell Squad: Cruz*

"Hell Squad is a terrific series. Each book is a sexy, fast-paced adventure guaranteed to please." – Amazon reviewer, review of *Hell Squad: Gabe*

Don't miss out! For updates about new releases, action romance info, free books, and other fun stuff, sign up for my VIP mailing list and get your free copy of the Phoenix Adventures novella, *On a Cyborg Planet.*

Visit here to get started:
www.annahackettbooks.com

Chapter One

"We're losing him!"

Dr. Emerson Green ignored her nurse's cry, gritted her teeth and kept working. Her gloved hands and arms were covered in blood up to her elbows, as she focused on saving the man on her operating table. "More blood."

Norah Daniels, the most reliable nurse on Emerson's team, worked to pump blood into their patient.

Emerson stared up at the glowing screen of the high-tech monitor attached to the man. It was one of only two that had survived the alien invasion and she was grateful they had it.

"Come on," she urged. He wasn't responding. He was bleeding somewhere, but she couldn't damn well find it.

"Max, can you isolate any sources of bleeding?"

The surgical robot beside her moved one of its four slender arms. "Negative, Dr. Green," the robot's modulated voice intoned. "The extent of the foreign damage is hampering my abilities."

Emerson leaned over the patient's open belly. She stared at the ugly damage the aliens had done to him—cutting him open, burning, scoring—carrying out their obscene tests. She had no idea what the aliens were trying to accomplish in their horror labs, but the patients the human commando teams had managed to rescue all had hideous injuries they'd have to deal with for the rest of their lives.

Not to mention the nightmares.

Emerson had tried to put them back together, to heal them. But some of them would always have scars—visible or not.

Her safety glasses fogged and she cursed under her breath. "New glasses."

Another nurse hurried to change out Emerson's glasses. There was some problem with the base ventilation. She knew the tech team was working on fixing it, but these things took time. Keeping a hidden underground base full of survivors running was a full-time job and their solar-power system was overloaded on most days.

"His pulse is dropping."

Dammit. There was too much blood. The extensive scarring and fresh injuries were hiding the problem, and no matter how much she searched, she couldn't find it. The muscles across her shoulders were stretched to breaking point. "Give him a shot of noxapin. A hundred mil."

When Norah didn't obey, Emerson looked up. "What's wrong? Come on."

The woman's round, dark-skinned face was tense. "We're almost out."

Noxapin was a highly experimental drug that

hadn't finished trials before the aliens had invaded. But it had been magic at keeping people alive long enough to survive surgery. Emerson had counted herself lucky that the medical supplies they'd scavenged had included it.

But they were almost through their stores, and clearly no one else believed this man was going to make it.

"Give it to him." She wasn't damn well giving up. On anyone.

They kept working. Emerson worked around Max as the robot's arms, with their different attachments, helped her. Emerson was in charge of the base's medical teams, it was her responsibility to do everything she could to help and heal anyone who was sick or injured. She mightn't be out on the front line, fighting the dinosaur-like raptors, but this was her way of fighting. Sewing people back together, saving their lives, pumping them full of nano-meds when their bodies were too injured to heal themselves.

Except whatever the aliens had done to this man had changed him so much that the tiny medical robots, that could heal a person in just hours, had stopped from working.

But she refused to give up. She'd been treating wounds and putting people back together ever since she'd first seen the huge alien ship blotting out the night sky over Sydney. Images flashed behind her eyes. She and her colleagues at the North Sydney Private Hospital had run up to the roof as soon as the ship had been spotted. An ugly, almost animal-looking thing.

Emerson had had a prime view when the small raptor ptero ships had poured out of the mothership and rained down on the unsuspecting humans below.

Most of whom had died.

Well, she damn well wasn't losing this one. She kept working, clamping, cauterizing, cutting out damaged tissue. She barked out orders for the surgical robot, for equipment, blood, more drugs.

"Emerson? Emerson?"

With aching tiredness dragging down on her, she looked over at Norah.

"He's gone, sweetie."

That's when Emerson's brain registered the constant shrill tone of the monitor.

She looked down. The man's face was relaxed, his skin pale. A dramatic contrast to the bright red of his blood all over her hands.

Sorrow dug into her like a burrowing worm. It knew just where to head to inflict maximum pain. "Time of death, 5:35 pm." She deactivated Max, the robot's arms slowly lowering. She stepped away from the table.

Another life she hadn't been able to help. She let herself feel the full punch of the pain, the anger, the sorrow and the failure. Then she shoved it down.

She couldn't afford to wallow in it. There were always more patients, more injured, more people depending on her.

As she tugged her gloves off and scrubbed her

hands, she relaxed the tiniest fraction. She loved her job, even when it sucked. Being a doctor...it was her calling. Before the invasion, she'd loved the high-pressure atmosphere of the ER, and had grand plans for her career. After a short time dabbling with surgery, she'd committed herself to emergency medicine. She'd loved the pressure, loved the idea of running her own ER one day.

Perhaps she should have been careful about what she wished for. Because now, she was in the ultimate high-pressure job and, for better or worse, she was the boss of medical.

Limited equipment, a motley mix of staff with varying backgrounds, and an unending stream of sick and injured.

She rubbed her now-clean hands against her face. She needed some coffee. Needed to get this nagging tiredness to take a hike.

Sleep would be best, but that wasn't going to happen. She hadn't slept well for two weeks.

As she hit the tiny kitchenette in the corner of the infirmary to make her coffee, a lump lodged in her throat. She'd spent too many nights lately in a lather of sweat, fighting back screams.

Damn raptors.

She thought of the man who'd died on her table. He'd been the one who deserved nightmares about their alien aggressors, not Emerson. She'd been their prisoner for maybe an hour. Sure, they'd beaten her, but she'd survived.

Hell Squad had rescued her. And the team's toughest soldier, Gabe Jackson, had held her as she'd cried.

Emerson sipped her coffee. She didn't deserve to have flashbacks and be traumatized by what amounted to nothing by most of her patients' standards. The caffeine hit her bloodstream. Much better. Still, if she didn't get some sleep soon, she might need to consider a sedative.

Nope. Her entire body rebelled at the thought. Not an option. If she got called out of bed in the middle of the night—which happened on an awfully regular basis—she needed all her senses sharp, not fuzzy from drugs.

She spun, walking past the line of infirmary beds. Currently only one bed was occupied—by a teenager with a bad case of the flu. It was a minor miracle. She'd recently gotten all the raptor-experimentation patients cleared to live in their own quarters in the base. Most had to come back for regular monitoring and treatments. But, for their recovery, being in their own space was important.

"Doc!"

Emerson jolted, Norah's shout almost making her spill her coffee. "What?"

"Hell Squad's on their way in. One of them is injured."

Emerson's heart stopped. Squad Six, also known as Hell Squad, was one of the base's commando squads. Every day the squads—made up of any soldiers and officers from any and all branches of the military and police forces who'd survived the initial alien attacks—went out to do reconnaissance, rescue survivors, protect the base and fight the aliens.

Hell Squad was the roughest, toughest and deadliest of the squads.

They mowed through aliens like a laser scalpel.

"Who's injured?" she asked, setting her coffee down.

Norah bustled around to get Exam Room One ready. "The scary one. Gabe."

Emerson felt as though the floor had shifted beneath her. She pressed a palm to the wall. *He'd be fine.* Nothing could keep Gabe down for long.

The doors to the infirmary burst open and Emerson turned. Gabe was being carried between two other men—Marcus, Hell Squad's leader, and Cruz, the second-in-command. The muscular men had their arms around the bigger, taller Gabe. Thankfully, their black carbon-fiber armor had a built-in, light exoskeleton that helped with lifting, because at six and a half feet of tightly-packed muscle, she knew Gabe wasn't light.

She stared at his blood-splattered face, her stomach clenching. Turbulent gray eyes looked back at her. He was alive, conscious, and mostly on his feet—that was what was important.

"Over here." She pushed back the curtain and waved them in. Norah hovered nearby. Emerson gestured at the nurse with a jerk of her head. "Finish up, Norah. I can take care of this."

The woman raised her brows. "Okay. Not going

to argue with you, Doc. Phillip is on duty tonight and in the office if you need help."

"Thanks." Phillip was a paramedic, and he, along with his boyfriend, Rick, were key parts of her medical team. Emerson yanked the curtain across.

"Not sitting on the fucking table," Gabe growled in a low voice.

"You'll do as ordered," Marcus growled back.

Hell Squad's leader had a voice that sounded like gravel and a scarred face that went with it.

"Chair," Gabe insisted.

Emerson pursed her lips. He was scratched up, deep gouges in his armor. *Through his armor.* She hissed in a breath. What the hell had gotten through his armor?

"Just put him in the chair," Emerson bustled forward. She didn't have time for them to have a pissing match. "Cruz, out."

The lean, handsome man stepped back far enough to be out of the way, and crossed his arms over his chest. "I'll stay. You might need help to hold him down. Or beat sense into his rock-hard head." His accent—American with a large dose of Mexican—had driven most of the base's single females into fits of delight, until he'd up and paired himself with a woman almost as dangerous as Hell Squad. The single ladies were still in mourning.

Emerson huffed out a breath. "Fine. Just stay back." She moved to Gabe and stepped between his legs. She pulled her portable m-scanner out of her lab coat. It was getting a little dented and was prone to shorting out at inconvenient times. Noah Kim, head of the tech team, had repaired it multiple times already, but he'd warned her it was on its last legs.

She ran the scanner over Gabe. "What happened, big guy?"

"Raptors."

She rolled her eyes. Gabe was a man of few words, but still. "I've never seen them tear through armor."

"Idiot went off half-cocked." Cruz's voice sizzled with anger. "Tore into them like Rambo."

"I was—"

"You should have waited for the team." Marcus did not sound happy.

The scanner beeped, and as she read the results, the tightness in her chest loosened. No major damage. Some minor blood loss, and some very deep gouges that had to hurt like hell. "You're lucky. You won't need surgery, just a small dose of nano-meds."

His impassive face didn't change, but she got the impression he wasn't happy about even getting nano-meds. The microscopic machines had revolutionized medicine fifty years back. A dose could heal a person in hours, instead of days or weeks. But they needed professional medical monitoring, or they could get out of control and wind up killing the patient.

She touched the jagged armor. "Let's get this off."

He sat still and silent as she leaned over his

broad shoulders, stripping the armor off. She felt the heat pouring off his dark skin. Marcus held out a hand and took the armor from her. When she stepped back and finally got a good look at Gabe's injuries, she hissed. They appeared far worse than the scanner indicated. The left side of his chest was a bloody, ragged mess of scratches. In one, she swore she saw the flash of rib bones. "Gabe."

"It's fine."

She grabbed her pressure injector, dialed up a painkiller, and before he could protest, slammed it against the side of his thick neck.

Gray eyes bored into hers.

Cruz had a handsome face, but Emerson found Gabe's so much more compelling. She'd seen his medical report, so she knew his father had been African-American. His skin was a deep, dark bronze, and with his shaved head, strong features, and storm-gray eyes, he was worth a second or third look. But he also radiated a menacing, dangerous intensity that had most people searching for a hiding place.

Gabe didn't appear to notice or care. Apart from with his squad members, he didn't socialize.

And since he'd lost his twin brother to the raptors almost three months before, he'd withdrawn even more. That dangerous edge turning razor sharp.

She grabbed some sterile cleaning pads and set to work washing the blood away.

"He gonna live, Doc?" Marcus asked.

"Yes. The nano-meds will have this healed up in

an hour or so."

"You got lucky, Gabe." Marcus shook his head. "You've held it together this long, don't lose it now."

Gabe remained stubbornly silent.

"The last two weeks, you've been taking more and more risks in the field."

Emerson's eyes widened. *What*? Since that mission to recover the patients, and her moment of captivity?

Marcus crossed his muscular arms. "You're going to get hurt worse than this, or get yourself killed."

Gabe's jaw worked. "I'll do what I have to do to take down as many alien bastards as I can."

Marcus slammed a closed fist into the exam table, the metal rattling. Emerson jumped.

Marcus' face twisted. "If you don't care if you die, think of your fucking team, then. You'll get one of them killed if you keep this up." Hell Squad's leader turned and stormed out.

Cruz shot Gabe a sympathetic look. "Get your shit together. I've said it before, and I'll say it again. If you need to talk, I'm here." He nodded at Emerson and left.

Emerson prepared the nano-med injection, measuring out the correct dose. She hooked a monitor up to Gabe. "Is what they said true?"

"I don't want to kill myself."

His voice was toneless and her heart tripped in her chest. He might not want to commit suicide, but he didn't much care if he died, as long as he took out as many raptors as he could when he did.

"Zeke wouldn't want this—"

"I don't want to talk about him."

The fierce growl made her sigh. "Fine."

Gabe gripped her wrist. "I'm going to kill every single damn raptor in Sydney. That way the one who shot Zeke and the ones who fucking beat you black-and-blue will be dead."

She couldn't look away from him. They stared at each other, the silence stretching between them.

Then he released her. "Do it."

The thought of him taking reckless risks, getting himself killed, had her anger spiking. She jabbed the injector into his arm harder than she should have. He grunted.

She watched the metallic-silver liquid drain from the injector, the tiny machines powering into his blood stream.

His gaze never left hers. She saw the muscles in his neck strain and he gritted his teeth. His body tensed, his back arching slightly. The nano-meds hurt on the way in, and right now they were replicating fast, traveling through his bloodstream and targeting the areas that needed healing.

"You keep taking risks out in the field, you'll end up dead." She wanted to touch him, to smooth a hand down his stubbled cheek. She shoved her hands in her lab coat instead.

"Don't need a lecture," he rasped between clenched teeth.

No, he wanted very little from her. She'd learned that the hard way. "Zeke wouldn't want this." She raised her voice. "Phillip?"

"Yes, Doc?" The tall man appeared, peering around the curtain.

Emerson shoved the electronic tablet at him. "Please monitor Mr. Jackson's nano-med infusion. Don't let him leave until you say he can."

Phillip cast a dubious look at Gabe, as if weighing up their differences in height and weight. "Okay."

"I'm off to grab something to eat." And shower the day's hardships away. She cast a final glance at Gabe.

He was staring at the floor.

If he wanted to kill himself, there was nothing she could do about it. Her heart hurting a little, Emerson strode out of the infirmary.

Chapter Two

Emerson stepped out of the shower, shivering a little. Goose bumps covered her skin and she quickly grabbed a towel and dried off. They had hot water for most of the day now, which was a huge improvement on the two hours a day they'd had for most of the last year. But when the base's solar-power system couldn't handle the load and they had to conserve, hot water was the first thing to go.

She fluffed her chin-length, blonde hair. She knew Noah and his team of electronics wizards were working to get more power for the base. One of the patients who'd survived the raptors' experimentation, Dr. Natalya Vasin, was helping. She was some kind of genius energy scientist. Emerson was just happy to see Natalya keeping busy and doing something she enjoyed. It helped with her healing—and that woman needed a lot of healing.

Emerson wrapped the towel around her body, deciding to make a cup of tea. She'd already grabbed a meal at the base dining room on her way back from the infirmary, so she wasn't hungry. Although, she suddenly remembered that she did have a block of homemade chocolate a patient had given her. That would definitely go down well right now.

She wondered if Gabe had finished healing. Nope, she wasn't going to think about him. She hitched her towel tighter. She had some patient medical notes she wanted to go over, and Noah had managed to find her some medical journals on genetics she wanted to take a look at. It wasn't her area of expertise, so the journals might help her work out just what the hell the raptors were trying to achieve when they cut those poor humans open.

Emerson stepped into her darkened bedroom. Since she was head of the medical team, she'd been given slightly larger quarters than the standard rooms most people lived in. Her bedroom was separate to her living quarters, with a rare, queen-sized bed. In the adjoining living room, she had a couch, tiny kitchenette and a corner she'd turned into a study. She spent most of the time—when she wasn't in the infirmary—at her desk, going over medical notes, or working on replicating drugs that were rapidly dwindling in supply. They'd scavenged what they could from nearby hospitals and pharmacies, but unless they could replicate what they had, they'd run short in months.

Her stomach cramped. *No.* She'd find a way. She wouldn't stop until she did.

Her gaze landed on the empty bed, its neatly-made covers mocking her. Reminding her of just how alone she felt. For a second, she wondered what it would be like to come home to…someone.

Emerson rubbed her temple. It wasn't like her to

wallow in melancholy. She had too much to do to sit around feeling sad and sorry for herself.

She took a step toward her small closet when a shadow moved in the darkened room. Her heart leaped into her throat. A tall, man-shaped shadow.

He moved toward her and she stayed still, her gaze glued to him, her heart hammering. She had no idea how he got in whenever he came to visit her. She knew her electronic door lock was engaged. She never heard him come into her room. He moved silently, like a ghost. And he never said a word.

Gabe stepped in front of her. He'd showered, his dark skin still damp, and he smelled like plain, simple soap. His well-worn jeans hung low on his hips, and his shirt was open, baring a muscled chest and rock-hard abs. No scratch or a scar marked the expanse of bronze skin.

Her heartbeat was like a drum in her ears.

He dropped to his knees in front of her.

Heat raced over her skin. She felt caught in a spell.

One big hand reached up and tugged the towel away, dropping it at her feet.

Then he pressed his face to her belly. His stubble scratched over skin, electrifying her. He breathed in and she reached her hands up, tracing the dark tattoo that snaked up the back of his neck with her fingertips before pressing her palms to his well-shaped skull.

He glanced up and the look in his tumultuous gray eyes made her breath catch. Naked, raw, primal need.

His hands slid down her sides and he backed her up a step until she felt her shoulder blades hit the wall. Then those big hands gripped her thighs and pushed her legs apart. *Oh, God.* Anticipation snaked through her. He dragged his face against her smooth belly and sensation rocketed through her. Everything inside her turned molten hot.

He dropped kisses on her hipbone, lower. Then he put his mouth on her.

God. His hot tongue delved into her folds. He knew exactly where to lick, where to suck, to drive her out of her mind. She trembled, not sure she could stay upright. Her hands blindly grabbed his shoulders, her nails digging into his skin. She heard sharp little cries and realized they were coming from her own throat. He kept working her, not letting up the hard pressure that was driving her insane.

He spread her legs wider, pushing one thigh up onto his shoulder. Then his tongue swept over her sensitive clit and she cried out. She was getting wetter and wetter, and pleasure was pulsing through her, growing to unbearable proportions.

She dropped her head back against the wall, staring at the smooth concrete ceiling of her bedroom. His mouth closed over her clit and sucked.

"Oh, oh..." She jerked against him. His hands clamped on her hips, holding her in place for his sensual assault. She felt one of his hands leave her hip and a second later, a thick finger delved inside her.

Emerson shattered. Her body flew apart in pleasure and she sobbed out his name.

Gabe caught her, rising and pulling her into his arms.

As usual, he didn't say a word. In the two months he'd been coming to her, appearing in the dark of her room without a sound, sliding the blankets off her and touching her, making her come over and over, he'd never said a word. And he'd never once acknowledged in public the things they did together in the darkest, loneliest parts of the night.

And nor had she.

He let her go and shrugged out of his shirt. Next, he unsnapped the button on his jeans. Emerson's gaze zeroed in on his hands. She watched as he unzipped the jeans and shucked them off. He wasn't wearing anything underneath, so she had the perfect view of deep-bronze skin and a long, thick cock that was more than a little intimidating in size. Her mouth went dry.

Unable to stop herself, she reached for him. But he caught both her wrists with one hand and gently pushed her hands away. Her jaw tightened. He never let her explore him. He'd touched every inch of her but he never, ever allowed her the same privilege.

Then his hands were on her hips, lifting her up like she weighed nothing, his palms sliding under her bottom. She wrapped her legs around his waist.

She felt the brush of his cock between her thighs and all thought rushed out of her head.

She had no idea what the hell was going on between them, but she knew she wanted him with a need that bordered on desperation.

***

Gabe looked at Emerson, her pale skin gleaming in the faint light coming from the other room. She was like a beacon pulling him in.

As it did every time he was with her, that tight, hot ball of pain, rage and grief that lived inside him shrunk, easing back a little and letting him breathe.

He pressed her back against the wall and the head of his cock brushed her slick folds. He swallowed a groan and watched her tongue dart out to lick her lips. Her skin was still damp—from her shower as well as the slightest blush of perspiration from when he made her come. Her normally sunny blonde hair hadn't yet dried, and it was shades darker than normal. It was slicked back, showcasing that interesting face of hers. She wasn't beautiful, but she was attractive with a sharp jaw, and bright-blue eyes and full lips he thought about far too much.

He could taste her on his lips and he wanted more.

Needed more.

He took a brief second to admire her curves. And

boy, she had good ones. She usually had them hidden beneath her sensible trousers and white lab coat. Damn that coat. He always wanted to strip it off her...or see what she might look like wearing only skin beneath it.

Gabe wasn't sure when this obsession with Dr. Emerson Green had started. Maybe the day he'd met her, when he'd gone in for his first medical checkup not long after coming to Blue Mountain Base. Or maybe one of the many times she'd patched him or one of the squad back together. Or perhaps it had been when he'd lost Zeke...and something inside him had broken.

Whenever it had begun, it had driven him to the one thing he'd known deep down could keep that ugly darkness in him at bay. Lately, the only time he could think clearly was when his cock was lodged deep inside Emerson's hot, tight warmth.

He pushed her thighs apart and moved until his cock rubbed against her damp folds. She cried out, arching into him. Damn, she was wet. All that slick desire, just for him. The head of his cock slid inside her. He took his time, thrusting in just another inch, using every ounce of his control to stop from slamming into her. He was a big man and he knew that he had to take it easy, let her adjust to him. She cried out again, her hands clenching on his shoulders. He'd have scratches tomorrow. Who knew that logical, smart Dr. Green was a wildcat in bed? He loved seeing the marks she left on him, and hated when they faded.

She tried to lower herself down on him, but he

held her in place, pushing inside only another tortuous inch. God, she was tight. He took his time, slowly easing in farther and farther. With one final slide, he was seated all the way. She gave a long moan.

Now, it was time to move.

He felt it building, that driving, desperate feeling. The need to possess her. Claim her.

He starting thrusting. Her nails dug into him again, her legs clamping around his waist. Soon, Gabe couldn't think. He just thrust into her, his gaze moving to her face.

Her skin was flushed, her upper teeth biting down on her full bottom lip. She arched into him, and in her eyes he thought he saw the same desperate need he felt inside him.

"Oh, God." She tensed and then her orgasm hit her. She screamed and as her body clamped down on him, Gabe's own release roared through him.

He thrust again, deeper, harder, and poured himself into her.

He had enough sense to stumble the few steps to the bed. He lowered them both onto the mattress, dropping most of his weight to the side, but still leaving her partly pinned beneath him. He buried his face in her hair and rode the blessed wave of bliss of feeling nothing but good.

One of her hands stroked his back. He took that to mean he was forgiven after her little snit in the infirmary. He had to kill the raptors, it was a driving imperative he couldn't ignore.

And he knew his strengths and weaknesses.

Knew he was built to take a lot of damage. He knew he could take down a hell of a lot of them. Maybe not the exact one who'd shot his brother, or the one who'd left Emerson beaten and sobbing in Gabe's arms. But others would die.

Remembering the horrifying quadcopter crash and waking to find her missing, his arms tightened around her. It had been a few of the worst hours of his life. He and the rest of the squad, injured, on the run behind enemy lines, and he'd had no idea if Emerson was alive or not.

Until he'd seen her on her knees in the dirt before a raptor commander.

But Hell Squad had kept fighting, and Gabe had gotten her out. He hated seeing a woman's tears, and Emerson's heartbreaking sobs that night had almost broken him.

Yeah, he knew what he was good at. Killing. The United Coalition Army had made sure of that. First with his training, and later with the experimental enhancements they'd made to him.

He also knew he wasn't good with people, especially women. In the past, when he'd needed one, he kept it to a hard, fast fucking and then he left. Most people knew he was dangerous, sensed it the way small animals did when a predator was around, and he was fine with people avoiding him.

But Emerson had never looked at him like that.

He thought, for a minute, about pulling her close in his arms and sleeping beside her. Maybe talking a bit.

But he knew he couldn't do it. He let her go and

slid out of the bed. He was dangerous, and anti-social. She didn't need him messing up her life. If he had real balls, he'd not sneak back into her bed again. As he dressed, he felt her gaze on him. He didn't say anything. What was there to say? It was safer for her if this...entanglement didn't get worse.

He shouldn't come back, but he knew he couldn't help himself. When that ugly ball of pain in him got to be too much to bear, when it was choking him, he always ended back here. In her arms.

He turned to leave.

He heard her sigh. "Gabe."

Gabe hesitated, then he walked out. He wouldn't stay. Couldn't stay.

Besides, it wasn't like she ever asked him to, anyway.

***

Emerson lay in the dark, still naked, the scent of sex clinging to her skin and Gabe's seed drying on her inner thighs. She heard her front door shut and she closed her eyes.

She felt... God, she didn't know how she felt. Sad, angry, confused.

Sex was a biological function. But she knew it gave people much more than that. Since the invasion, people's attitudes toward sex had changed. Casual sex wasn't frowned upon. It was a way to feel close to someone, especially when most people had lost their loved ones. It was a way to cope with the stress of their lives, and a way to continue the human race. Not that she had many pregnant women. Most were too afraid to bring a child into such an unsettled world. But soon the contraceptive implants most people had would start to wear off. It was up to Emerson to devise a way to replicate them, give people the choice if they wanted to start a family in the middle of an apocalypse.

She sighed and rubbed her face. Gabe was just coming here for a release. That much was obvious. It was clear he didn't even want to talk to her.

And just because she was confused and feeling upset about it wasn't his fault.

She sat up and spied something on her bedside table. A single flower. A beautiful white lily.

Oh, Gabe. God, the man confused her. She picked up the flower and breathed in its scent.

Not relishing another night of raptor-induced nightmares, or sensual dreams about a man who was close but at the same time so far out of reach, she got out of bed.

Her desk was waiting and she had work to do. And it helped her ignore the raw pain inside.

Chapter Three

"Hey, Bryony. Nice shirt." Emerson smiled at the young girl and waved her into the infirmary.

The ten-year-old shot her a shy smile. Her dark hair was cut very short due to the fact that the raptors had shaved half her head and drilled into her brain. But she was recovering nicely. Her shirt was olive-green with Hell Squad stenciled on the front of it.

"Cruz got it for me." The girl turned her head to look up at the man behind her.

Cruz shrugged a shoulder. "Wouldn't fit me."

The woman standing beside him snorted. "That girl has you wrapped around her teeny tiny finger, Ramos. She could ask you for a tropical vacation and you'd get it for her."

As Emerson ushered the trio inside the exam room, she thought Santha's observation was right. But while the soldier might be deeply fond of the small girl, his heart very clearly belonged to the tall, slim woman with him.

Santha Kade had survived alone for months, living in Sydney's ruins, fighting back against the raptors any way she could. After helping Hell

Squad, she and Cruz had teamed up to rescue human prisoners from the raptors' labs. And those prisoners had included young Bryony.

Since then, Santha had moved into the base with Cruz, and was now heading up a new reconnaissance division. She and her small team were sneaking in and out of raptor territory and feeding intel back to the squads.

But it was the way Cruz looked at her, like she was his end and his beginning that made Emerson's throat close.

She looked away and focused on her patient. "Okay, hop on up here, Bryony." Emerson patted the exam bed. "I'm going to check you out."

The girl hopped up, her sneakered feet swinging. "I'm feeling better."

"Good." Emerson gently tilted the girl's head, studying how well the bone was being repaired by the regen therapy she'd used. "Do you like your new room?"

"Oh, yes. Santha's helping me decorate."

Behind the girl's back, Santha grimaced. "I'm doing my best."

Emerson hid her grin. She guessed a former SWAT-team member didn't have much interior-decorating experience.

"And Cruz and Marcus smashed down a wall."

Emerson's eyes widened. "They what?"

Cruz smiled. "We put a door in so Bry's new room is linked to our place."

As Emerson clicked on her m-scanner, she felt a surge of happiness. To see two tough warriors like

Cruz and Santha take a young girl under their wing…

"Your vitals all look good. Today, I'm going to run a more in-depth scan on your head. Okay?"

"Will it hurt?" Bryony's voice held the slightest tremble.

Damn the raptors. "No, it won't hurt." Emerson swung the larger resonance scanner around on a flexible arm. "I'm just going to put it near your head. It'll make a little humming noise and send a picture to that screen there—" she pointed at the comp screen "—and you won't feel a thing."

Santha grabbed the girl's hand and squeezed. "When you're ready, Bryony-girl."

Bryony looked at Santha, then Cruz. "You'll stay?"

"For as long as it takes," Cruz promised.

Bryony straightened her thin shoulders. "I'm ready."

"Good." Emerson turned on the scanner. "It'll take a few minutes, so just relax. Anyone need a drink?"

Santha and Cruz shook their heads.

"I'm okay," Bryony said.

"Hell Squad off today?" Emerson asked casually.

"Yeah." Cruz crossed his arms over his chest, the tribal tattoos on his arms visible under the edges of his T-shirt. "Everyone needed a bit of downtime. They're in the gym, beating each other up. It's Reed, Claudia, and Shaw versus Gabe. Marcus is refereeing."

Emerson stilled. "Three against one?"

Santha made a noise in her throat. "Yeah, they should have made it four against one. Gabe is super strong and super deadly."

A scowl took over Cruz's face. "And lately...well, Gabe's gotten even more intense, more driven."

Emerson's stomach turned over. Yeah, he was very clearly winding tighter and tighter, and when he finally snapped...

"How are you, Emerson?" Santha asked quietly.

"Fine. Busy."

"You were trapped with the raptors and took quite a beating—"

"All recovered." She smiled, and wondered if it looked as brittle as it felt.

"Yeah, physically, maybe. But it takes time for the wounds inside to heal, for the terror to fade."

Santha's quiet tone resonated with understanding. Emerson knew the woman had been forced to watch her sister be attacked by raptors, and later dealt with the shock of finding her dying in a raptor lab.

But Emerson knew Santha threw herself into her work fighting the raptors.

And Emerson was doing the same thing, albeit on a different battlefield. "I'm really okay."

The other woman didn't look convinced, but before she could talk again, the scanner beeped. With a frown, Emerson turned her attention to the monitor.

What the hell? She studied the screen, and tapped it, double-checking the odd result.

"Doc?" Cruz asked.

"There's..." She glanced at Bryony, not sure if she should bring this up in front of her. But steady, pale-green eyes stared at her. Eyes that had already seen too much and seemed far too aged for a ten-year-old. It was Bryony's head, and after everything she'd been through, she deserved some honesty.

"There's something lodged in your head."

Santha gasped and slipped an arm around the girl.

Anger flashed over Cruz's face. "What?"

Bryony swallowed. "But my head doesn't hurt, and I feel okay. So, what is it doing there?"

"I don't know." Emerson felt like such a failure with that answer. Despite treating and monitoring all the lab survivors, she still didn't know exactly what the aliens had done to these people, or why. Yet.

She tapped the screen, running an analysis on the object. She frowned again.

"It appears to have a crystalline structure." She looked over the girl's head at Santha and Cruz. "The computer says it's made of the same substance as the information crystals the raptors use to store information on."

Cruz cursed.

Bryony glanced up. "Naughty word, Cruz."

"Sorry." He pinched the bridge of his nose.

"Doc Emerson?"

Emerson crouched down to Bryony's level. "Yes, sweetheart?"

"I want you to take it out."

"I think—"

Bryony shook her head hard. "No. I want it out." Her tone was firm.

Emerson released a long breath and looked at the couple. "I think I can remove it. It's very close to a hole in her skull. It's likely how they inserted it in the first place."

Cruz pressed his hands to the back of his head. Santha touched his arm. "We both trust the doc. More importantly, Bry trusts the doc."

Emerson looked at the little girl. "I'll have to put you under for the procedure."

A tear slipped down the girl's cheek, cracking Emerson's heart. But she nodded.

"All right." Cruz ruffled Bryony's short hair, then his gaze hit Emerson's, liquid-brown eyes drilling into her. "Do it."

***

Gabe hated being on base patrol. He much preferred to be blasting aliens.

He walked through the trees, his carbine in his hands, keeping an eye out for anything unusual. The base was hidden in the Blue Mountains west of Sydney. Standing here, in the peaceful tranquility amongst the trees, you couldn't tell a fucking alien apocalypse was raging only miles away.

He stepped over some rocks and saw a flutter of bright color. A rainbow lorikeet swooped down from the trees, landing on the grass near a rock, completely unaware it was sitting right near an entrance to Blue Mountain Base. The base's entrances were well hidden, all blending into the natural scenery to avoid detection. It also helped that the raptors seemed to hate being amongst trees.

"Nice day, huh?"

Gabe eyed his partner. Reed MacKinnon was the newest member of Hell Squad. A former United Coalition Navy SEAL, the tall, rangy man had outdoorsman stamped all over his rugged, tanned features. He was apparently magic in the water, not that they got the chance to go in the water much, and Gabe had seen firsthand that the guy was damned good with explosives.

And he was also Zeke's replacement.

Gabe grunted in reply. He didn't hold it against the guy, but every time Gabe looked at Reed, he thought of his dead twin.

"You know, mostly we're doing night infiltrations, wading through raptor blood, or dodging raptor poison." Reed took a deep breath. "Fresh air and sunshine are a nice change." His gold-colored gaze fell on Gabe. "You gotta take the good when you can get it. Helps you shake off the bad."

Gabe looked away. "Yeah."

"How's the doc?"

Gabe barely contained his jerk. "What?"

"Emerson? I haven't seen her much since that fucked-up mission. She was hurt pretty bad."

"She's healed. Always in the infirmary, helping someone, performing surgery." She seemed fine.

But Gabe would never forget her swollen, black face. Or her nightmares and screams the few days after. She'd been so shaken lying in that infirmary bed that he'd stayed beside her the entire time. Holding her hand when she'd woken in a cold sweat.

He wondered if she still had the nightmares. Each time he'd visited her, she'd seemed okay. Tired, but okay.

"Seems like a workaholic to me. Hiding behind work."

Gabe frowned. Hell, that did sound like her. Thoughts crowded into his head. Damn, he hated patrol. He kicked a dead branch that lay on the ground. There was no time to think when you were firing at raptors.

"We should check the solar array," Reed suggested.

They worked their way over to the solar-power system. At first, the trees in the area just looked like the rest of the bush. But when you looked closely, you could see that the veins running through each leaf were actually wires. Each leaf was a tiny photovoltaic cell.

They wandered around. Everything was quiet, and it was making him antsy. He'd much rather be on a quadcopter heading into the city. Actually fighting the aliens, not soaking up the sunshine like they were on some damn picnic.

He heard footsteps heading in their direction. He stiffened. Quiet ones, still a little way off. "We've got company."

Reed straightened and cocked his head. "I don't hear anything. You're damn spooky when you do that."

Yeah, Gabe's hearing was enhanced, as were his strength and endurance. It made some people nervous. He listened to the approaching steps. "Two people."

Reed clutched his mayhem, a modified carbine with a mini-explosives launcher attached. "Raptors?"

"Nope. Human. Women."

"You can tell?"

"Too light for a man."

A second later, two women dressed in fatigues emerged from the trees. He instantly recognized Mackenna Carides, the second-in-command of Squad Nine. She was tiny, wouldn't even reach Gabe's shoulder, but she was all tightly-packed muscle with a tough disposition. She'd even tossed him on his ass once when they were sparring. Not many men could do that, let alone a woman. Yep, Mac was not someone to mess with.

The other woman was of medium-height, with dark, red-streaked hair. She carried her carbine like she knew how to use it, and she had a face that wouldn't have been out of place on the beauty magazines he knew some of the base's women traded like gold. She was all cream skin, large, whisky-colored eyes and long dark lashes. She was another Squad Nine member, but he couldn't remember her name.

"Gentlemen," Mac said with a nod.

"Out for a stroll, ladies?" Reed asked.

"We've come to relieve you. Marcus wants you down in Ops."

Gabe straightened. "Something up?"

"Something. But I don't have the details. We were just told to take over your patrol and send you down."

"Thanks," Reed said. "We've just covered the southern quadrant and we were headed east."

"Got it," Mac said.

Gabe nodded at them before heading for the closest entrance back into base. It was a disguised hatch that opened to reveal a ladder heading downward. He and Reed descended, their boots ringing on the metal. They navigated the tunnels until they reached the Operations Area. It was always a buzz of activity. The main room was filled with comp screens on the walls and desks. A mix of military staff moved around, monitoring drone feeds, coordinating operations. It was known as the Hive.

"Gabe. Reed."

The feminine voice made them both turn. Elle, Hell Squad's communications officer, was waving them over to a conference room.

"Hey, Elle," Reed said.

"Hi." She had a bright smile that lit up her pretty face. Her dark hair was tugged back in a ponytail. Once a Sydney socialite, her family had been killed in the first wave of the invasion and she'd had to trade her designer wardrobe for fatigues. But she was a damned good comms officer. "We're in here."

Oh, and she was also Marcus' woman. Gabe would never have picked it. Small, slender Elle and rough, scarred Marcus. But to Gabe's surprise, they seemed to fit each other, like two pieces of a puzzle.

Marcus and the rest of Hell Squad were waiting. As was Emerson.

Gabe drank her in. Her hair was in its usual neat bob, blonde strands brushing her jaw. She wore her white lab coat, and she didn't meet his gaze, but she was busy chatting with Shaw, Hell Squad's sniper.

When Emerson let out a laugh, Gabe scowled. Shaw was also a notorious ladies' man.

The door opened and another man strode in. General Adam Holmes was the head of Blue Mountain Base. Gabe had heard some of the squad members grumble about him. The man was military through and through, his khaki uniform always pressed, his dark hair always neat. Gabe actually liked him. From what Gabe had seen, the guy dedicated everything he had to keeping the base safe, and humanity fighting back against the alien invaders.

"I got a call that this was urgent," Holmes said.

Marcus nodded. "The doc found something."

Emerson stepped forward. "This morning, I was running routine checkup scans on one of the raptor lab survivors, Bryony."

A few gazes swung toward Cruz. He was standing, arms crossed, looking pissed. Everyone knew he and Santha had practically adopted the young girl and were protective of her.

"The scan revealed something lodged in her brain," Emerson said.

"Fuck," Shaw breathed.

"I removed it."

"She okay?" This from Claudia, Hell Squad's only female member.

"Couldn't be better. Recovering and milking it for all it's worth," Emerson said with a small smile.

"Ice cream," Santha added. "Kid will do anything for ice cream."

"What was the item you removed?" Holmes asked.

Emerson nodded at Elle. An image appeared on the large comp screen on the wall.

Gabe frowned. It looked like a small chip of black crystal in a perfect square.

Elle took over. "It's made from the same crystal the raptors use to store their electronic data."

"Got anything off it?" Holmes said, frowning at the screen.

"Not yet, we're waiting for Noah—"

The doors slammed open and a man strode in. Noah Kim was dressed in black today. With his long black hair brushing his shoulders and his high cheekbones, it made him look like a fucking pirate. He was actually some sort of genius, with a crazy-high IQ, and the ability to make computers dance to his tune. He was also in charge of comp systems, the drones, and helping with the power systems.

"I got something off the chip." He rattled off some file names to Elle. A second later the image on the screen changed. "The item is a smaller version of their data crystals." He scowled. "It was recording the girl's bio data—"

"The girl has a name," Cruz growled.

Noah held up his palms in an apologetic gesture. "Right. It was storing Bryony's bio data."

"That would be useful," Emerson said. "The...tests they were carrying out, they wouldn't need to constantly monitor her. Just wait a set period of time, then remove the chip."

Noah nodded. "It also stores visual images."

Marcus leaned his hands against the table. "Things she saw?"

"Yeah. I've never seen anything like it." Noah tapped at the comp screen on the table. "But I think you'll find the images interesting."

The pictures flashed up. They were a bit blurry, distorted. But clear enough.

Some were of humans lined up in beds, tubes running from different parts of their bodies. Gabe took a deep breath. It was the lab where they'd rescued the girl and some others.

There were raptor faces. They might be humanoid in shape, but their faces were pure alien. Thick, gray-mottled, scaly skin covered large, hairless heads. Their features were heavy, their jaws elongated and their mouths full of teeth.

Then the pictures showed something new.

Everyone in the room gasped, or hissed in breaths.

It showed large tanks, hundreds of them, all in rows.

"What the fuck?" Marcus said.

Shaw moved forward. "We saw tanks like these in the second lab. The one at Luna Park. But there were only three of them."

And they'd had humans floating in them.

Gabe cursed under his breath, remembering something else from the other lab, too. When Marcus had yanked the poor people out of those tanks, they'd died instantly.

Chapter Four

Gabe watched image after blurry image of the tanks flash across the screen.

"It's not over." Santha stared at the screen with a mixture of shock and incandescent anger on her face.

Gabe knew her sister had died in one of these labs.

"Stop there," Emerson said.

Elle stopped the slideshow. "Is that—?"

The image showed the equivalent of a raptor comp screen beside one tank—large and black.

"Those scrawls and scratches, that's text, right?" Emerson moved closer. "Elle, can you translate it?"

They were slowly building up their knowledge of the raptors' language, and Gabe knew Elle was one of the best at deciphering it.

"I think..." Elle tapped and swiped the screen of her tablet. "Yes. It says Genesis Facility."

"Genesis," Emerson murmured. "Let's see the last few images."

They saw other human prisoners being moved through the lab. Bryony must have touched one tank, because the image showed a small hand pressed against the glass, the shadow of a human body floating inside it.

Gabe's jaw tightened. Goddamned fucking aliens.

The image changed again and suddenly, Emerson gasped. The tablet she was holding clattered to the floor. Gabe frowned, and before he realized what he was doing, he took a step toward her.

She was staring at the screen, a closed fist pressed to the base of her throat.

The image showed a raptor. This one looked slimmer than a standard raptor soldier, his face narrower. He was missing an eye. It looked like it had been gouged out; thick scars crisscrossed the empty socket.

"Emerson? Are you okay?" General Holmes asked.

She shook her head and looked away from the screen. Her gaze caught Gabe's for the briefest second. Tears shimmered in her eyes. It was like a punch to his gut. Emerson rarely cried.

Then she straightened and faced the general. "That's the raptor who was responsible for...guarding me during my short-lived captivity."

Gabe's jaw clenched so tight he thought the bone would splinter. "That's the fucking raptor who beat you?"

One short nod.

"You're sure, Doc?" Marcus asked. "They all look pretty much alike."

"I'll never forget," she whispered. "His eye..."

Yeah, that missing eye and the ridge of darker-gray scar tissue were pretty distinctive. Gabe curled his fingers into his palms, forming fists. The fucker was going to die.

"I think...I think he might have had something to do with the labs. I obviously couldn't understand their language, but he was really angry that Hell Squad had sprung his prisoners."

Gabe slammed a fist on the conference table. "We find this facility, we go in, and we do what we do best—blow it to hell."

Behind him, he heard his teammates murmur their agreement.

Emerson drew herself up and turned to face him. "Not yet. I need to get as much of their research as I can, first. I have to work out what they're doing to us. If they're searching for weaknesses, developing biological weapons, I need to know. It could help the people they've experimented on, and it could help others around the world. I doubt this experimentation is only happening here."

General Holmes nodded thoughtfully. "We've been trying to get messages out to the other human enclaves. Warn them about what the raptors are doing." He looked up at the image. "Anything else we can get would be very helpful."

Emerson nodded. "And I need to see those tanks."

No. Gabe blinked. He couldn't believe what he'd just heard her say. "You can't go in there." He stabbed a finger at the screen. "Remember what happened last time?"

A flash of pain crossed her face, and fuck, he hated himself for putting it there.

"Yes. I remember. But that doesn't change anything. I have people to help."

"You can't be—"

"Gabe." Marcus cut him off, a hard look matching his hard tone.

Gabe bit off a curse.

"Of course, we need to *find* this…Genesis Facility, first." Marcus' gaze swung over to Santha.

The tall woman stepped forward. "My team is still finding its feet, but we'll start looking straightaway."

Gabe looked back at the scarred face of the raptor. He was going down. The ugly fucker would feel Gabe breathing down his neck. A surge of anticipation raced through him. He'd wanted a target for his rage, and he'd just found one.

The base alarms sounded and everyone in the room went on alert.

Holmes touched the nearest comp. "Raptor patrols spotted heading a bit too close to base." He looked up, his gaze direct. "Hell Squad, you're relieved of patrol duties. Get out there and take down some raptors."

As Gabe followed his team out, he looked at Emerson.

She watched him, her chin up, her eyes defiant.

Yeah, well, he knew he had to stay away from her…for her sake. But that didn't mean he wasn't going to do whatever he had to do to keep her safe…whether she liked it or not.

***

The infirmary was quiet. It was late, most of the base was asleep in their bunks.

Emerson shifted her tablet on her workbench, watching as the results of her latest tests came in. The lab was tucked away in a small room in the back corner of the infirmary. She stared at the glass beakers and tubes filled with various colored liquids—solvents, chemicals, bodily fluids, blood. She'd tried to sleep, but the nightmares had hit. Her heart thumped, beating a little faster at the memories. She did *not* want to spend a night tossing and turning, or worse, hiding out in her bathroom trying to outrun the memories.

She grabbed a syringe, sucked up blood taken from a patient, then squeezed it into an empty test tube. She added the tube into her analyzer, forcing her attention on the machine, determined to block out the memories. She had no right to be so haunted by her brief encounter with the raptors. Not when so many others had suffered far worse. But she could hear the raptor grunts, their guttural snarls, heard the slap of fists on flesh. And boy, she remembered the pain.

Glass shattered.

Gasping, Emerson stared down at the beaker she'd knocked to the floor. *Dammit.*

Whenever she was struggling, she did what helped take her mind off the bad. She thought of Gabe. She slipped her hand in the pocket of her lab coat and pulled out the polished stone she'd found sitting on her desk in the infirmary.

It was a beautiful, deep green. She rubbed it between her fingers. She was getting quite a collection of them. She'd find them on her desk in her quarters, here in the infirmary, one slipped in the pocket of her coat.

That day when he'd lost Zeke, she'd been so worried about Gabe. The twins had been close, they'd had a bond that was clear to see.

She'd always been drawn to Gabe. At first, because she'd been curious about his abnormal test results. The army had done *something* to him, although in typical Gabe fashion, he'd stubbornly refused to talk about it. But her tests didn't lie—he was faster, stronger, had better vision, better hearing.

But once you looked past the scary, he was a gorgeous hunk of badass man. With his shaved head, lickable dark skin and silver-gray eyes.

Mostly, she loved his quiet intensity. He didn't rush to speak for the sake of it. When he did talk, he made intelligent observations. So yeah, Emerson had found Gabe Jackson attractive from the day she'd met him.

He was so incredibly different from the men she'd dated before. Not that she'd dated much. Her career had been her focus and busy, crazy, insane ER hours hadn't left much time for nookie. She'd had a friends-with-benefits arrangement with a colleague. God, she missed Michael sometimes, and while she'd never had confirmation, she suspected he'd been killed when the raptor ptero ships had bombed the hospital. Mike had been a clean-cut, busy doctor like herself, with a quick laugh and an easy-going nature. She'd loved him as a friend and their chemistry was good.

But not off-the-charts, blow-her-mind chemistry like with Gabe.

She'd never thought Gabe had noticed her as anything other than a doctor—just a part of the team that supported the squads.

Until that night after his brother had died.

She had woken from her sleep, heart pounding, and known someone was in her room.

She'd seen a large, dark shadow and a second later, she'd smelled him—dark musk and sexy man—and known it was Gabe.

He hadn't said a word. He'd just leaned down and kissed her. She shivered at the memory, her hands curling around the edge of her workbench. A hard, intense kiss. Then he'd yanked her covers back, stripped her naked and made her come—on his fingers, with his tongue, and then he'd spread her legs and pounded inside her.

Emerson closed her eyes. God, even now she was getting turned on. He hadn't stopped until dawn. She'd been limp and exhausted by morning when he'd slipped away without a word.

And all the other nights he'd done the same.

She pinched the bridge of her nose. But she finally admitted to herself why Gabe twisted her up and left her so confused.

She wanted more.

Oh, God. She closed her eyes. She wanted more from Gabe Jackson and she wasn't sure he wanted the same. Or was capable of giving her what she needed.

Dammit. She dropped her hand and focused back on the workbench. She had work to do.

There was a whisper of sound and she spun.

Like she'd summoned him, Gabe stood just inside the door of the lab, his burning, gray eyes locked on her.

Chapter Five

Gabe didn't know why the hell he was here. He kept telling himself he had to stay away from her, but he just...couldn't.

Emerson stood, looking at him, all neat and proper in her lab coat.

Finally she moved, bustling over to him. "Are you hurt?" Her gaze drifted over his armor.

Fuck. He was hot, sweaty and he stank of raptor blood. Shouldn't be here.

He'd torn into the raptors they'd attacked. Taken down almost all of them single-handedly, until Reed and Cruz had pulled him back. Marcus was pissed at him again, making threats about kicking Gabe off the team.

The thought was a punch to gut. He *needed* the team. They were all he had left.

Them and the smart, beautiful doctor standing in front of him.

Emerson started patting him down. "The blood doesn't appear to be yours. Anything hurting?"

Yeah, but nothing she could see. And nothing anyone could fix.

He yanked her close, wrapped his arms around her and buried his face in her hair.

She went stiff for a microsecond, then relaxed against him. Her arms wrapped around his waist. "Oh, Gabe." A quiet murmur.

He held her. Thinking that she smelled like citrus and disinfectant. He'd always loved oranges and limes, and hell, even disinfectant was starting to smell appealing.

As long as it was coming from her skin.

Finally, she pulled back. She pointed to a door. "There's a bathroom through there. Clean up."

Shit, he'd gotten raptor blood all over her lab coat. With a nod, he went. He stripped his armor off, took a quick shower in the tiny stall and used a too-small towel to dry off. There were some clean sets of scrubs on a shelf, but there was no way in hell the trousers would fit him. Thankfully his cargo pants had escaped too much damage under his armor. He did pull on a green shirt from the shelf since his T-shirt was soaked in sweat and blood.

When he came out, she was at her workbench, wearing a clean lab coat, scribbling something on a tablet. She raised her head, looked him over, and her lips twitched. "You do *not* look like a doctor." She tilted her head, her smile widening. "Hmm, maybe a stripper dressed as a doctor."

Gabe wanted to squirm. A stripper? No one had ever, *ever* accused him of that.

She nodded her head to a nearby table. "Eat."

Gabe sat and eyed the tray. The food had been nibbled on and he figured it had been her dinner. He frowned. Why the hell hadn't she finished it?

He studied her, watching her as she worked. God, he loved her steady, efficient movements as she touched the tablet, studied the comp screen, then squirted stuff into test tubes.

She was damn smart. Only in her early thirties and running the entire medical team for the base. He picked up the fork, and realized he was starving. He attacked the remains of her protein substitute, potatoes and salad. And he just kept watching her. He realized he could happily do that all night.

"I'm running tests on blood from some of the raptor lab survivors." She spun, setting tubes into a circular machine that blinked with a bunch of different lights. "I *am* going to work out what the hell those aliens were trying to achieve."

She didn't appear to expect him to reply, so he kept eating and watching. He'd never noticed the way her eyes narrowed and she bit her bottom lip when she was concentrating on something. He stared, fascinated, at those neat white teeth sinking into the plump flesh.

"Were they just testing us for weaknesses? Looking for a way to annihilate everyone who's left?" She shook her head. "I've seen the scope of the things they've done. It has to be more than that. Maybe they're using us as Guinea pigs to test their own medical tech?"

"Or weapons," he said.

She paused. "Maybe. Biological weapons." She tapped some notes into her tablet.

She carried on talking about what she was

doing, and Gabe felt the tension easing out of him. Her voice, her presence, was so soothing.

But soon he felt another tension growing. As he watched the gentle sway of her hair against her jawbone, and the way those teeth kept sinking into her lip. *Shit.* He shifted on the stool. When she bent over, her lab coat settling over her shapely ass, he almost groaned. Emerson had curves, ones that fit perfectly into his big hands. And he knew he wasn't the only one who'd noticed. His jaw tightened. She was his, dammit. No one else was getting close enough to touch her.

His cock was hard, pressing against the zipper of his trousers. He needed her.

Now.

He moved over to her. When she stepped back and bumped into him, she gave a little yelp.

"Dammit, Gabe. You need to make a bit more noise when you move." She ran a hand through her hair. "In here, you aren't in the field, sneaking into raptor territory, so you don't have to be all stealthy and..." Her gaze met his and her words trailed off. Her cheeks flushed.

He reached up and started undoing the buttons on her shirt.

She licked her lips. "What are you doing?"

"Pretty sure it's obvious."

"Someone could come in."

It wasn't likely. It was the middle of the night and besides, he'd locked the lab door on his way in. If there was an emergency, the alarms would give them ample warning before anyone found them.

He pushed her shirt open, but didn't take it off. He wanted to keep the lab coat on her, too. He'd dreamed of fucking her with that maddening coat on. She was wearing a pink satin bra that cupped her lovely breasts. Those plump mounds were rising and falling with her quickened breaths.

He unsnapped her trousers and shoved his thumbs in either side of the waistband. He took her trousers and panties to the floor. His cock spasmed, making him groan. Damn, she was beautiful.

He lifted her up and she wrapped her legs around his hips with a breathy cry. Gabe took a few steps to an empty bench away from her work and set her down on it. He stood between her open thighs.

"Gabe." Her voice trembled.

God, just her saying his name made him harder. He needed to be inside her. Feel her wrapped around him. But first, he wanted to hear those little noises she made when she came.

He shoved the bra down, lowered his head, and sucked one nipple into his mouth. She arched her back, pressing into him. Her hands shaped his head, clutching at him. He lapped, tugged gently with his teeth. He knew exactly how much pressure she liked. He switched to the other plump breast.

Then he let one hand drift down her gently rounded belly. Emerson was a study of contrasts. A razor-sharp mind, but the rounded, curvy body of a goddess.

Perfect.

His hand found the nest of blonde curls between

her thighs. He brushed her clit, rubbed it. She made an inarticulate cry, her hips moving, seeking more.

He sank a finger into her warmth. She was so wet for him. He thrust in and out, added a second finger, feeling her stretch around him.

"Oh, yes." She was panting now.

But Gabe decided he wanted to see her come with him inside her. He lifted his head, pulled his fingers out of her.

"No!" She grabbed at him. "Don't leave me. More. I need more."

He gripped her thighs, pushing them apart. Her mouth dropped open.

He quickly wrenched open his trousers, circled his cock with one hand, then rubbed it against her. Her gaze was glued to his erection, watching it against her paler skin.

He pushed just the head in, watching her stretch to take him. Her eyelids fluttered, her cheeks flushed. Her heels dug into his ass. He slowly inched inside her, making sure she watched his possession of her.

Finally he was all the way to the root. He stayed there, savoring the feel of her.

Then he pulled back and thrust back into her with one smooth stroke. She cried out, her hands gripping his shoulders.

He pumped into her, hard, fast and forceful. A rhythm he knew would get them there quickly. He gripped her hips to hold her in place. Flesh slapping against flesh. Jesus, he felt his own release growing, coiling inside him. He let one hand slide down to find her clit, rubbing the tight nub as he thrust inside her.

With a hard arch of her back, she came, crying out his name.

It startled him. It was the first time she'd ever said his name as she came. And it drove him over the edge.

With a loud groan, he emptied himself inside her.

He stayed there, leaning against her, his face pressed to her neck. He felt so good. Damn, his legs felt like glue. He pulled in some deep breaths.

As always, the perfect peace he found in her arms started to dissipate. He looked over her shoulder, and spotted some medical files on her comp screen. Pictures of what the raptors had done to their prisoners.

Shit. He'd come to her, covered in raptor blood, death on his hands. The darkness in him writhed. He needed to leave her the hell alone, before the ugliness in him spilled over onto her. Before she saw just how dangerous he was. He didn't ever want to hurt her.

He needed to stay focused on what he did best.

He pulled out of her and tucked himself back inside his trousers.

When he looked back, she was watching him silently. It was then he noticed the bruises. On her breasts. Her thighs. All in the shape of his fingertips. Fuck, he lost himself in her and forgotten his own damn strength. He knew better.

He had to find the will to stay away from her. He was out there, fighting the raptors, for Zeke, but also for Emerson. Even more so since she'd been hurt by them.

And he'd kill himself before he saw her hurt by his hands.

He pulled his zipper up and stepped backwards.

She held out a slim hand. "Stay."

Something inside him weakened. Resolutely, he took another step back.

"I need more, Gabe. Talk to me. I know you're hurting. Give me something, anything."

He felt a muscle tick in his jaw. For her sake, he had to find that strength.

But turning and walking away from her was the hardest thing he'd ever done.

***

Emerson lifted the m-scanner off the middle-aged woman. "Everything looks great, Priya."

The woman nodded. "I'm feeling good, too." She glanced around the infirmary. "And I'm so grateful to be here at the base and not…" Her voice drifted off.

Emerson patted the woman's shoulder. After the horror of the raptor lab, she figured Blue Mountain Base was like a paradise.

She eyed the slowly-fading scars scoring Priya's arms. "You keep putting the med gel on those scars and they'll be gone in a few weeks."

"You got it, Doc Emerson." Priya stood.

"Thanks." She nodded her head at the open lab door. "How are all those fancy tests going?"

"Slowly." But Emerson's throat felt dry as dust. She stared into the lab, her gaze falling on the empty workbench. She swallowed. In that instant, all she could think about was Gabe's big body moving thickly inside hers. The all-consuming way he made love to her.

Made love? She scoffed at herself. Gabe Jackson fucked her. For relief, to pound out his pain and frustration. Actually, she had no idea why he came to her. It wasn't like he took the time to talk to her, tell her how he was feeling.

"Nothing much to report, yet."

With a nod, Priya left. Emerson turned and eyed the last few patients sitting on the chairs in her makeshift waiting area near the door. One was standing, pacing a little as she waited.

Dr. Natalya Vasin had been painfully thin when Hell Squad had pulled her out of the raptor lab. But Emerson had been pumping her with high-calorie supplements, and the woman's face and figure were starting to fill out. Her dark hair had been shorn off, but she'd had it cut and shaped by someone in the base and now her hair accented her long, slim neck and made her look like a pixie. But what Emerson guessed was slowly leaching the anxious, worried look from Natalya's face was working with Noah and the tech team. She clearly loved her work as an energy scientist and was helping boost the base's current power systems.

"Natalya." Emerson waved her into the exam room.

The woman shook her head. "No. Someone else can go." Her voice held the faintest Russian accent. "Look, Doc, I really am fine. I don't need a checkup."

Natalya's anxiety poured off her in waves. Emerson knew the woman still had violent nightmares of the lab. Her scar was still visible, peeking out of her neckline, ugly and red. She'd refused treatment on it. Refused to let Emerson help much at all. Emerson had scanned her when she'd first arrived to check for anything dangerous, but apart from that, the scientist refused any further examinations.

"Natalya—"

A violent shake of her head. "I've been poked and prodded enough." Her voice hitched. "They cut me open, scanned me, all against my will. This is my choice. No more tests, or scans or procedures."

Emerson's shoulders sagged. "Okay," she said quietly.

With a nod, Natalya turned and ran out of the infirmary.

Emerson sighed. Natalya had also refused to talk with the base therapist, but Emerson might just have to force the matter. She turned to the remaining patients. "Okay, Helen, you're up."

The distant peal of alarms rang. She dragged in a breath and wondered if Hell Squad were headed out.

Norah popped her head out of the office. "Doc?

Call for you. I routed it to your comp."

"Thanks. Excuse me, Helen. I'll just be a minute." Emerson entered her office and tapped her comp screen. Marcus Steele's tough, scarred face filled the screen.

"Doc. One of Santha's team found the Genesis Facility."

Emerson gripped the comp screen. "You're sure?"

"Saw tanks with human bodies floating in them. Sounds like the right place."

"You're heading out?"

"Yeah. And I need you to suit up. We might have survivors who need medical attention, and you wanted to see the tanks."

Her chest tightened. "I'm on my way."

Chapter Six

Emerson strode toward the Hawk landing pads. She was in her black body armor, with her small black backpack full of medical supplies slung over her shoulder.

The landing pads were always busy. Mechanics bustled around the Hawk quadcopters, while other Hawks were landing or taking off. They'd lost one on the mission to rescue the final lab survivors and that had been a serious blow. They were obviously impossible to replace.

She saw Hell Squad milling near a Hawk, checking their weapons.

As she walked over, her gaze went to Gabe. His head lifted, his face impassive. She looked away. God, it hurt to look at him.

"Doc." Marcus stepped forward.

"I'm ready."

"Good. Hell Squad, let's move."

Marcus helped her into the Hawk. She settled into a seat and strapped in. Cruz sat nearby, looking alert and ready.

"You are such a moron." Claudia Frost swung her carbine over her shoulder, her hot gaze on the team's sniper.

Shaw rolled his eyes. "Will you get off my case, Frost? I don't need your bitching today."

"Bitching?" Claudia's tone turned Arctic.

Reed was watching them, grinning. He looked ready to grab a tub of popcorn.

Marcus took a menacing step forward. "Not now. You can both bitch at each other when we get back. Right now, I need you focused."

Gabe was standing near the back. He finished checking his carbine, then grabbed a handhold dangling from the ceiling.

"Hold on, Hell Squad." The pilot looked back from the cockpit. From what she'd heard, Finn Eriksson was the best Hawk pilot they had. He'd broken his arm in the Hawk crash and he hadn't been happy that she'd had him on restricted duties while he healed. But he was back in fighting—or rather flying—form, now.

The quadcopter lifted off. They ascended through a vertical tunnel of rock. Out the window, she just caught a glimpse of the overhead doors retracting. Once they were airborne and clear of the tunnel, the Hawk spun, the four rotors tilting, and they flew east toward the city.

The sun was shining and it was such a beautiful day. Emerson really needed to try and get outside a little more. They had set times people could head topside, with an armed patrol. But she did have a few who were too afraid to leave the safety of the base and needed vitamin D boosters.

Marcus had left the Hawk's side door open and air rushed past. As they reached the outer limits of the city, her chest tightened, like it always did when she saw what had been done to her home.

Rubble and ruin.

That was pretty much all that was left of the once-bustling capital of the United Coalition—the union of several countries including Australia, the United States of America, India, Canada and several European nations. Sydney had thrived, been a place to share knowledge, do business, holiday and see amazing culture. She'd always loved that it was such a melting pot of people of different backgrounds and histories.

She sighed. *Gone.* And it wouldn't be coming back. Just like the shining career she'd had before the aliens came. She'd had such grand plans, had wanted to help so many people.

She set her shoulders back. She was still helping people. The world was changed, different, but the core values were still there. Every day, she saw courage, tenacity, hope and love.

Her gaze strayed to Gabe. A lot of things weren't what she'd planned or thought she'd want, but it didn't make them any less real.

"Okay." Marcus stood, his tough, muscular body silhouetted by the sun streaming in the door. "The facility is located in a still-intact skyscraper in North Sydney."

"Not far from the Luna Park lab," Cruz said.

"Yeah. We'll land one klick away, move in and take down any raptors we encounter. So far, Elle says the drones have only picked up one small patrol."

Emerson touched the tiny earpiece in her ear. Elle would feed them whatever intel they needed.

"Okay, we're landing in three minutes. Hell Squad, ready to go to hell?"

"Hell, yeah," the team yelled. "The devil needs an ass-kicking!"

Soon, Emerson felt the Hawk start its descent to an overgrown patch of green lawn below. She watched the team press the buttons on the neck of their armor and retractable helmets slide into place. She did the same. Her stomach flip-flopped and she breathed deeply. She always felt nervous, no matter how many missions she came on or how many badass soldiers surrounded her.

"You got a weapon?"

Gabe's deep voice rumbled in her ear. She looked up.

Damn, this close, his gray eyes were mesmerizing.

"I have a small laser pistol. But I shouldn't need it with Hell Squad around me."

"Out there, anything can happen. Keep the pistol close." He went silent, staring at her. Then he lifted a hand, it hung there between them for a second, then he touched a finger to her cheekbone.

She sucked in a breath. He'd never touched her in public before.

"Stay safe out there, Doc."

When he pulled back to stand with Cruz and Reed, Emerson noticed Claudia watching her with a keen gaze. The dark-haired woman shot her a sharp smile.

Emerson swallowed and gripped her backpack. The Hawk touched down.

"Go, go!" Marcus waved them out.

Soon Emerson was jogging toward a tall building ahead, surrounded by Hell Squad. They always kept her in the middle when she was in the field. She didn't like the idea of them being human shields for her, but she'd seen them fight. They'd take down anything trying to get to her long before it reached them.

"You should be in visual range now of the building's main entrance." Elle's voice was calm and steady. "Directly ahead, five hundred meters."

Emerson saw it. Large glass doors into a lobby. She glanced around. As far as she could see, everything was still and silent, and there were no signs of raptors. Wrecked cars lined the street, and rubble lay strewn in all directions.

Marcus reached the doors first. He unclipped something off his belt and pressed it to the glass. A light blinked on the small metal circle. A second later, she saw it glow red-hot.

The glass started melting.

Soon, the doorway was just a gaping hole, the glass a melted puddle on the ground. Hell Squad waited.

"Elle, anything?" Marcus murmured.

"Nothing on screen. You're clear to enter."

Inside, the lobby looked normal, seeming to be untouched by the invasion. Marcus waved them toward the stairs.

"You need to get to the third floor," Elle said. "It

used to be a gym for the building, and Santha's people said that's where the tanks were spotted."

They moved up through the dark stairwell, clicking on the tactical flashlights attached to their carbines. Six beams of bright-white light cut through the darkness.

"Here we are." Marcus pushed open the door.

Inside the room was dark as well. It appeared most of the windows had been blacked out. Emerson got the sense of a cavernous space.

The flashlights fanned through the darkness. Illuminating a cavernous *empty* space.

"Fuck," Marcus cursed.

Emerson stepped around him, her heart beating hard. She saw round marks on the ground, pressed into a rubber floor that had obviously been part of the gym. Objects with circular bases had sat here very recently. The rows of marks stretched off into the darkness.

The tanks were gone.

***

Gabe stared at the empty room. Everything was gone.

He saw something glittering on the floor and stepped forward. Glass. He crouched and touched a finger to it. It wasn't like any glass he'd seen before, it was a pale amber with faint vein-like striations running through it. Raptor tech had organic components integrated with it. He guessed a tank had broken on the way out.

Then Elle's voice cut across the comms. "Raptors! Hell Squad you have raptors incoming."

Marcus cursed. "Hell Squad, ready for—"

A door slammed and raptor fire tore through the space.

The team dived for cover, returning fire at the same time. Green raptor poison splattered on the rubber floors, sizzling as it ate through it.

Gabe tackled Emerson around the waist. They hit the ground and he covered her body with his.

"Gabe, stay with the doc." Marcus crawled up beside them. "We'll chase these fuckers down." He yelled an order at the team, and in a precision move, they were up, running in a zig-zag pattern and firing at the far end of the room.

Suddenly a large door on the opposite wall opened, letting light in, and the shadows of retreating raptors could be seen running into another stairwell. Hell Squad reached the door and seconds later, followed them out.

Silence fell.

That was what combat was like. All hell breaking lose one minute, silence the next.

Hands pushed at his chest. "Can't...breathe."

Shit. He rolled off her and helped her sit. "You okay?"

"Yes." She looked around, her face hardening. "They're gone. Those poor people being subjected to God only knows what—"

"We'll find them."

She nodded but they both knew the reality. The longer it took, the more humans who'd be dead or suffering.

"I'm going to take a look around," she said.

He nodded, watching as she wandered around, crouching every now and then to study where the tanks had been. She walked past gym equipment—weight benches, treadmills and bikes—stacked against the far wall.

Gabe clutched his weapon. With his enhanced hearing, he could hear the team's carbine fire echoing in the stairwell. He also heard the faint guttural shouts of raptors. His fingers tightened on his weapon.

He wanted to be with them. He wanted to be killing raptors. Zeke would have laughed and told him to learn a bit of patience.

A stab of pain in the chest. Yeah, well, Zeke wasn't here.

A giant boom echoed up the stairwell, along with the shouts from Hell Squad.

Gabe tensed. His hands clenched on his weapon.

Emerson gasped. "Do they need help?"

He could hear the team firing, and heard their shouts through the earpiece. There were more raptors than they'd anticipated. He heard Shaw swearing. A raptor projectile had winged him.

"Gabe, go."

"No."

"I have a weapon." She flashed the little pistol on her hip. "And besides, there's not much shadows can do to hurt me."

He stood there, undecided. More than anything, he wanted to be down there tearing into aliens.

Emerson turned her back to him, studying the broken raptor glass. She pulled out a small camera. "I promise, I'll wait here."

Another boom and more shouts. "Okay. Stay near the stairwell doorway. You see anything strange, you hide."

"Go."

Gabe rushed into the stairwell. He ran as fast as he could, his boots pounding on the stairs.

He rounded a landing and saw the squad in the lobby below. Marcus and Cruz were fighting hand to hand with several large raptors, their combat knives glinting. Shaw and Claudia were pinned down, hiding behind the reception desk. He didn't see Reed.

A raptor leaped at Gabe and he swung the carbine around. The fucker was too close, so Gabe swung the butt of his gun and slammed it into the alien's face. As the raptor stumbled back, Gabe unloaded laser fire into the alien's chest.

Gabe lifted his carbine and strode into the aliens. He let his rage loose and fought.

Soon, the raptors lay dead around them.

"Thanks for the help, *amigo*," Cruz said, swiping an arm across his brow.

"What the fuck are you doing down here?" Marcus said.

"I heard it wasn't going well. Emerson sent me down."

Marcus snorted. "Sure. Wasn't like you were

jonesing for an alien kill."

Gabe stayed quiet, Marcus' words hitting a little close to home. Now the raptors were dead, he was anxious to get back to Emerson.

They marched back up the stairs and stepped in the gym.

Gabe frowned. Where was Emerson? There was no sign of her. His heart knocked in his chest.

"Doc?" Marcus said with a frown.

A growl echoed through the darkness.

"Fuck." Shaw swung his rifle up. "I hate canids."

The alien hunting dog slunk out of the shadows. It had tough scales, a razor-sharp row of spikes along its back and teeth that would make a megalodon proud. The canid's eyes glowed hellish red.

And its teeth were coated in blood.

No. Gabe strode forward, his mind emptying of everything except two phrases. *Find Emerson. Kill the alien.*

He fired, holding his finger down on the trigger. The canid danced out of range, its muscles bunching to attack. *Yeah, come on.* Gabe yanked out his gladius combat knife and leaped to meet the animal.

They slammed together. He felt teeth and claws sinking into his armor. But with every ounce of his enhanced strength, he shoved the knife into the canid over and over again. Side. Neck. Chest. Sometimes the skin was so tough he had to work it hard, sawing the knife in.

The canid made a final, high-pitched yowl before it died.

Gabe was up, striding to where he'd last seen Emerson. "Doc? Emerson!" If that thing had hurt her... He clamped down on the thought. He yelled her name again.

If she was dead...no, she couldn't be dead.

"Over here."

The sound of her voice washed over him and made him feel weak for a second. He rushed to the back wall.

He looked up. A built-in climbing wall rose from the floor up into the darkness above. Emerson perched half-way up it, clinging precariously to the handholds. And there was someone with her.

Gabe stood beneath Emerson, not remembering moving. "Let go."

She didn't hesitate. She let go and dropped into his arms.

"You're okay? It didn't touch you?" He saw streaks of blood on her armor and his hands tightened.

"It's not mine. I'm okay. It got my backpack and it attacked Jason here."

Gabe didn't look away from her beautiful face. She was alive. And unharmed.

"Ah, this is Jason."

She gestured to the man who'd shakily climbed down to join them. He was shaking, his skin pale and sheened with perspiration and blood.

"He managed to escape the raptors and hide so they couldn't find him. He saw the tanks, saw the raptors taking them out of here."

The man, in his early thirties, nodded.

Gabe turned back to Emerson, and finished looking her over.

"I'm okay," she said again, her face softening.

"No thanks to you, Jackson."

Gabe looked up. Marcus was wearing his "I'm pissed and you'll pay for it" face.

"You were told to stay here and protect her. You left her unguarded. She could have died...because of you."

Gabe closed his eyes for a second, his arms tightening on her warm weight. *Fuck*. Marcus was right. Things could have been very different and he could have been carrying her dead body back to the Hawk.

Just like he'd had to do with Zeke.

"I told him to go," she said. "You guys needed help."

"You aren't his leader," Marcus said darkly. "He had orders and he knows better."

Gabe set her down.

Marcus scraped a hand over his helmet. "You need to take some time and get yourself together, Gabe. Since Zeke died...you're taking risks you never would have taken before, just so you can spill some raptor blood."

Each word was like a laser blast to Gabe's skin. He straightened but didn't say anything. What the fuck could he say? It was all true.

"You almost got the doc killed—"

"Marcus—"

Marcus didn't let Emerson say another word. He chopped a hand through the air. "Don't defend him. This is my squad. I deal with it my way."

Emerson closed her mouth.

"You almost got her killed. Not the raptors, *you*."

The word hit Gabe like raptor projectiles. "Am I off the team?"

Marcus half turned and cursed. "No. But you're off offensive missions for now. You'll be on base patrol and training new recruits."

Which Marcus knew he hated. But Gabe figured it was far less than he deserved.

He felt like things were just spinning out of control. That the darkness inside was pulling him under.

An image of Emerson dead, her blue eyes unseeing, her skin covered in blood, made him feel sick.

His fault. All his fault.

Chapter Seven

As soon as the quadcopter landed back at base, Emerson called out to her waiting medical techs. They stood with a hovering iono-stretcher, and in moments they had Jason loaded.

"Get him settled. I'll be in the infirmary in a moment."

The man and the woman nodded and headed off.

Emerson glanced around the landing pads and spotted Hell Squad making their way out.

"Gabe."

He paused and turned, reluctance stamped all over him. His face was set in stone. "Not now, Emerson."

"Look, about what happened—"

"Don't want to talk about it," he bit off, his gray eyes stormy.

A flash of anger whipped through her. She set her hands on her hips. "You *need* to talk. You never talk."

He leaned down so no one else could hear him. "When I'm making you come, you don't need me to talk."

She narrowed her eyes. "Don't be crude. I want you to talk to me. Share the load. I can see you're holding stuff in, and it's hurting you."

He straightened. "Don't want to talk about it."

"Damn obstinate man," she muttered. "I'm good enough to sleep with but not to talk to, to share anything with. Is that it?" God, saying those words out loud hurt.

His jaw hardened. "Emerson—"

She shook her head. "You can't have it both ways, Gabe. Share with me, or stay away."

Something flashed in his eyes. "An ultimatum?"

Her stomach cramped. She'd never wanted it to come to this. She'd stayed quiet so long because she hadn't wanted to scare him away.

But that had been selfish of her. He needed help.

"Funny, you wanted me to share, spill all my demons, but who do you share with, Emerson?"

She went very still. "I don't know what—"

"You think I can't see you're fucked-up, too? What the raptors did to you, what you deal with and see every day in the infirmary. I know it leaves a mark. You still get nightmares?"

She looked away. "I'm fine."

"No, you just bury it under your work."

"I think we're done here," she said frostily.

His gray gaze ran over her face, like he was memorizing her features. "Yeah, I guess we are." He turned and stalked away.

Emerson felt herself waver, like she'd taken a punch to the stomach. So...this was the end. No more midnight visits. No more little gifts. No more Gabe.

She took a second, then pulled in a long breath.

She needed to get to the infirmary and give Jason a thorough health check. That was all she could think about right now.

She moved on autopilot, stripping out of her armor and heading to the infirmary. Her domain.

Soon, she was helping settle a freshly showered and fed Jason back into the pillows on his infirmary bed.

"Your heart rate is a little fast, Jason." Emerson frowned at the scanner. Not a surprise, really, considering what the guy had been through.

"I'm okay."

Everything else looked normal. He was still pale and sweaty, but he probably just needed some rest. "Look, you get some sleep. If you need anything, just let me know."

Emerson had just stepped back when the infirmary door opened. Elle's pretty face appeared. "Hey, Doc."

"Hi, Elle."

"I'm here to drag you off to the Friday Night gathering."

Emerson screwed up her nose. At the end of each week, a bunch of the base's residents packed the large rec room off the dining hall. People drank, blew off some steam, found someone to cuddle up to for the night. Tonight, she was definitely not in the mood. "I can't tonight. Besides, you know I never enjoy them."

No, even with her lab coat off, everyone saw a doctor. She got peppered with so many questions and requests, and it was never relaxing for her.

"I know. I have a plan." Elle smiled. "We'll sit with Hell Squad and they'll scare off anyone coming to ask you about strange rashes or bad backs."

Sitting with Hell Squad. Sitting with Gabe.

"You're...leaving me?" Jason's anxious voice broke through her thoughts.

He looked even paler, rubbing his hand across his mouth. With some rest, a few more meals and some sunlight, she suspected they'd find a handsome man under there.

"Everything's fine, Jason."

Elle's face turned serious. "You've been under a lot of stress, Emerson. You recently went through a bad situation, and had a near miss today—"

When Jason grabbed Emerson's hand, gripping hard enough to hurt, she was startled.

"Don't go."

"Jason," she soothed. "I'm not going anywhere." She gently disengaged his hand and looked at Elle. "I can't, Elle...I just can't."

It appeared something in her tone registered with the other woman. Elle eyed her with speculation. "Okay. Another time."

After Elle had left, Emerson plumped Jason's pillows. "I'll be right over there in the office. And I promise I'll come back and check on you before I head to bed."

He licked his lips. "You promise?"

She nodded and smiled. "Get some rest."

Once she was back in her office, she sank wearily into her chair. She stared at her desk.

There was no polished stone sitting on the shiny surface, no pretty flower gracing on her files, no shiny piece of fruit by her tablet. It was just her and her work.

She bit her lip, fighting back the choking loneliness. This would pass. She'd survived a long time without Gabe Jackson. She could do it again.

***

"Come into Dr. Emerson Green's House of Healing." Emerson waved Santha into the exam room. "I'll try not to stick you with too many shots."

Santha grimaced and pulled herself up on the table. Her resignation was like a wet blanket hanging over her. "That's not particularly comforting, Doc."

Emerson pulled the curtain. "You're tough, suck it up."

The other woman snorted.

"You look more scared than when you face down a pack of rabid canids," Emerson said.

"I wouldn't have come if a certain stubborn-ass alpha didn't bully me into it."

Emerson frowned. "What's wrong?"

"Nothing." Santha lifted one slim shoulder. "I'm just tired, feeling a bit off. I tried to tell Cruz that setting up a brand new intelligence team to spy on an invading alien horde is, you know, tiring."

Emerson attached a sensor clip to Santha's finger and tapped the comp screen, setting it for some standard readings. "Not to mention having a sexy soldier keeping you up at night."

The brunette's lips twitched. "You tell me to give up sex and I'll be ignoring doctor's orders."

Emerson laughed. "So, the alpha maleness is balanced out by the great sex."

"Oh yeah." Santha's face softened. "And the fact that he loves me." She looked bemused. "And takes care of me."

A burn of emotion lanced Emerson's heart. Gabe had, in his own way, tried to take care of her. Emerson shook her head. She couldn't think of him right now. The scanner beeped. "Hopefully we can avoid a prescription that involves no nookie."

Santha looked around the small exam room. "Actually, it's kind of nice to be out of the Intel Office for a little while. Gabe is driving me insane."

"Oh? Gabe is usually so…quiet."

"Yeah, but he looms and broods and demands. Over my shoulder, every minute of the day. He really wants this Genesis Facility found more than he wants to breathe."

The flicker of test results popping up on the screen caught Emerson's eye, but she ignored them to focus on Santha. "He's still dealing with Zeke's death. I think he lost the one person he could talk with. I'm worried. If he doesn't talk, let out all the festering emotions, well… He needs to accept his brother is gone and no amount of dead raptors will change that. I'm worried he'll…"

"Implode," Santha finished quietly, her pale-green gaze on Emerson's face.

"Or get himself killed."

"Yeah, the squad's worried about him too." Santha tilted her head. "You have feelings for him."

Emerson felt a rush of heat in her cheeks. "What? No, I—"

"I've seen the way you two look at each other." When all Emerson could manage was a strangled sound, Santha waved a hand. "Don't worry, I don't think Hell Squad knows. I've just gotten good at picking things up."

Yes, Emerson guessed a year alone waging war on aliens honed those kind of skills. Damn Santha's observant nature. "I...I...it's not easy having feelings, confusing ones, about someone who won't talk to you. He... Well, in bed we have no problem."

Santha smiled. "Oh, all that broody intensity. I bet still waters run deep."

"But out of bed, he can't, or won't, let me in. I think for him, it was just physical. Anyway, we're over now."

Santha eyed her for so long, Emerson wanted to squirm.

"Emerson, I saw him out there on that mission when the Hawk went down. When he came to and realized you were missing, we had to hold him back from charging into a mass of raptors to find you. And later, when he saw they had you...there was no way on Earth he was leaving without you."

Emerson's memories of the night were thankfully a little blurry. But she remembered Gabe charging through the fighting to grab her, and how he held her as she cried.

Santha grabbed her hand. "That man cares. He's

just not good at explaining himself, or how he's feeling. Must be a Y-chromosome problem."

Emerson gave a short laugh. "Testosterone."

"There you go."

"He leaves me little gifts sometimes. Flowers, fruit, small things."

Santha grinned. "Oh yeah, he cares."

The scanner made a series of beeps.

"All done." Emerson studied the screen. "Everything looks okay—" One line jumped out and Emerson blinked. "Well. I'm not sure how to tell you this..."

Santha stiffened. "God, have I got some virus?"

"You've got something. You're pregnant."

Now the woman went stone-still, her eyes saucers. "Come again?"

"Pregnant. Gestating. With child."

"No way." Santha pressed one palm to her flat belly and the other slapped against her forehead.

Emerson stepped closer, worried the woman was going to faint.

"I have a contraceptive implant. So does Cruz."

"Cruz is due for his to be replaced." Emerson grimaced. "I've been stretching the limits on their use-by dates because we only have a few left. When was yours due to be replaced?"

Santha looked up, clearly running some metal calculations. "Oh, God." Her face turned stricken. "A few months back. With everything...I completely forgot. And up until a few weeks ago, sex didn't feature in my life." Her face changed, the hard edges smoothing. "A baby. Cruz's baby." Then every drop of color leached from her cheeks. "I can't raise a child. Our planet's been devastated, it's dangerous, nothing's safe or certain." She looked up. "And I am not mother material."

"Don't panic." Emerson touched her shoulder, squeezed. "This baby will have you and Cruz to protect it. That's a pretty good start in my books. And you're doing a great job with Bryony."

"God—" Santha grinned "—Bry will love this." The grin melted away. "What if he doesn't want a baby? God, how am I going to tell Cruz?"

"Tell me what?"

Both women jumped. Cruz stood in the doorway, his tight white T-shirt stretched over his muscled chest and tattooed arms.

"Doc, is she okay?"

There was so much emotion in his voice— concern, anxiety, love. "Well—"

"Oh, God." Santha pressed her face into her hands.

Cruz got a panicked look on his face and strode to her side. "*Mi reina*, whatever it is, we'll deal with it. Together."

"Okay." Santha lifted her head, took a few deep breaths. "I'm pregnant."

He went tense. "Pregnant? With a baby?"

"Well, I hope it isn't a kitten."

"A baby." He breathed the words with reverence. "We're going to have a baby. Jesus, Santha." He yanked her into his chest and buried his face in her hair. "A baby."

Love. This was what it looked like. Emerson

pressed a hand to her chest. It was so damned nice to see it amongst the horror and terror she dealt with most days.

And she wanted it.

Boy, did she want it.

After they'd worked out a schedule for some wellness appointments, the couple left and Emerson headed back to her office. She had some files to go over and she needed to beef up the schedule for regular blood donations all the base residents had to give. Supplies were running a little low. But instead of work, she found herself just sitting there, staring into space. She wanted Gabe to look at her the way Cruz looked at Santha.

She just had no idea what she was going to do about it.

Work. She had work to do. Emerson plunged into her files like a woman possessed. When she lifted her head, her neck was stiff. She rubbed at it and eyed her watch. Hours had passed. She stared down at the medical file open in front of her. It was from one of the lab survivors. Some of his test results were strange. She'd need to run some new tests and investigate further.

But for now, she needed to check on Jason and get to her bed.

The lights in the infirmary had been dimmed, but the lamp was on beside Jason's bed. He was sitting upright, rocking back and forth, his face in his hands.

She frowned. "Hey, Jason."

"Dr. Green." He made a strangled noise and

moved fitfully. It was then she noticed he was covered in a sheen of sweat and his sheets were soaked.

"Jason? What's wrong?" She stepped closer.

He raised his head, one hand still covering half his face. "I can't fight it anymore."

Fight it? "Stay calm. Let me help you. I'll get you a sedative—" She started to turn.

"No!" He grabbed her wrist.

Sharp nails bit into her skin and she cried out.

When she looked down, she saw blood welling, dripping down her arm. His nails were long, pointed...like claws.

She looked back at him and he dropped his hand from his face.

Emerson's heart stopped. One side of his face was normal.

The other side was covered in gray scales.

And his eye glowed a demonic red.

"I'm sorry," he hissed. His mouth was filled with sharp teeth.

She tried to yank away from him.

He lunged, springing off the bed like an animal.

As he hit her, Emerson's scream echoed in the empty infirmary.

Chapter Eight

Gabe flicked through more drone footage. He'd been at it for—he glanced at his watch—hours. And nothing. Not a single clue as to where the aliens had moved the Genesis Facility. He'd seen plenty of raptor patrols, and raptors terrifying and killing human survivors. His hands clenched. Humans too far away from the squads for them to rescue and help.

He tapped the screen and brought up more feed. The drone team had dozens of the little machines out there, searching. He looked at the notes on the tablet beside him. Intelligence from Santha's team. They had a few hunches they were checking out. One guy, Devlin, was good. Damn good. He'd gotten right into raptor territory, close to their main ship, without being seen. Guy was either crazy, or very well-trained. He'd been pretty cagy about what he'd done before the raptor invasion...but Gabe had his suspicions.

Gabe went into his own directory on the network and made a new notation. An image file caught his eye, and he hesitated for a second before he clicked it.

A photo of himself and Zeke filled the screen.

Zeke. His twin had the same face Gabe saw in the mirror every day. But he hadn't shaved his head like Gabe, just kept his dark hair short. And his face had seemed more...open. Zeke had liked to joke and laugh. Damn. He'd been the best of them.

And he'd be fucking pissed at the risks Gabe had been taking. Even more pissed Gabe had gotten himself sidelined from active missions. Gabe ran a hand over his head. God, he wished Zeke were here.

Maybe Emerson was right. Maybe he was going to have to find a way to purge this...ugly blackness inside him. He stared blindly at his brother's image. Maybe Gabe had being doing this all wrong.

Emotions churned inside him. Damn, he needed to do something. Anything. Maybe he'd hit the gym, see if someone was up for sparring.

He checked his watch. Hell. It was really late. Everyone would be in bed.

He knew where he wanted to go. His port in the storm.

His jaw tightened. He should leave her alone. She'd make him rip the scabs off and he wasn't sure he could handle that. He also owed her an apology for being a dick at the landing pads.

Gabe headed out of the Ops Area. When he got to her quarters, he made short work of hacking her electronic lock. But the instant he stepped inside, he knew her rooms were empty.

There was only one other place she'd likely be.

He wandered the empty tunnels. Everyone would be sleeping, tucked up with their loved ones or with whomever they'd found to help stave off the loneliness.

He rounded a corner and spied a dark-haired woman running off down the tunnel. Reed standing there, watching her go.

When he sensed Gabe, Reed looked back over his shoulder. "Hey, Gabe."

Gabe raised a brow. "Bit late to be out." He eyed Reed's bare chest and the damp towel around his neck.

"Could say the same thing to you," Reed said.

"Been in Ops, looking for any sign of the Genesis Facility."

Reed shook his head. "You need to take a break sometimes, bud."

"Who was your friend?"

"Someone who needed a break." Reed stared down the hall, a troubled look on his face. "Sometimes I need to sneak out of here and get some fresh air. She did too."

Gabe knew Reed was an outdoorsman. A former UC Navy SEAL before the attack, he loved the water and always told them stories about hiking, surfing and mountain biking. Being stuck in an underground base had to drive the guy crazy.

"So...you headed to the infirmary?" Reed asked with the faintest hint of a smile.

Gabe stayed silent.

Reed shrugged. "Okay, keep your secrets, bud."

As Reed turned to go, something urged Gabe to talk. He grabbed the other man's shoulder. "Wait." He dropped his hand. Uncertain. "I...I like the doc."

"We all do. Smart, funny, hard-working, sexy. She's pretty likeable."

Gabe scowled.

Reed laughed. "I've got eyes, Gabe. Besides, I think your kind of 'like' is a little different than for the rest of us."

"She's—" *perfect* "—social, outgoing, friendly."

"Ah, clashes with the man-of-few-words thing? They say opposites attract."

Yeah, but Gabe wasn't so sure. Maybe opposites attracted, but could they stay together?

"I'm dangerous."

"We all are, Gabe." Reed held up a hand. "And I know you're...more...but I sure as hell know you'd never hurt a civilian." Reed eyed him thoughtfully. "You want my advice?"

Gabe nodded.

"Be honest and be yourself. If you're thinking something, just tell her. She doesn't expect sonnets and songs from you. I think she just wants you. Badass Gabe Jackson."

"What made you an expert on this...relationship stuff?"

Reed grinned. "I like women. All of them. Young, old. Pretty, plain. Straight and round. There's just so much to discover. And if you treat them right—" he winked "—they'll treat you right, too."

They said goodnight and Gabe strolled toward the infirmary. Okay, just be honest, tell her what he was thinking. He could do that.

The infirmary door appeared ahead. She'd be hunched over her desk, working. The woman worked too damn much. She had a team of doctors, nurses, technicians. She could take a break occasionally.

A crash sounded from inside.

Every muscle in Gabe's body went on high alert. He charged through the door and rushed inside.

His heart stopped. She was flat on the ground, a man on top of her.

Something washed over Gabe in a flash. Something dark and deadly. He stormed forward, not making a sound.

One step from them, the man looked up.

Fuck. Shock hit Gabe. Not a man. A raptor. Wait...not really a raptor, either. Some sort of hybrid?

One eye gleamed red, filled with angry hunger. His fang-filled mouth was covered in blood.

With a roar, Gabe grabbed him and yanked him off Emerson.

He swung the raptor-man around, and the sound of a growl filled the air.

Using his enhanced strength, Gabe flung him. The raptor crashed through two infirmary beds, tipping them over, before he hit the floor.

But a second later, he rose.

Then he bounded over the overturned beds and flew at Gabe.

Gabe was ready. Hand-to-hand was his specialty.

Gabe swung out. He hit the man—raptor, whatever the hell he was—in the face. The raptor spun, growling as he did. Gabe hit out again.

The raptor ducked. Damn, he was fast. Faster than a regular human.

But then, Gabe wasn't a regular human, either.

He kicked the man, hitting him in the gut. They traded a few blows, the man growling and snarling the entire time.

But he had one major disadvantage.

He had Emerson's fucking blood on his mouth. Gabe had no idea how badly she was hurt, but she was bleeding. This thing would pay for that.

Gabe snatched up a stool. He swung it in a wide arc, throwing all his power behind it. It slammed into the raptor's head.

The creature howled and fell on the floor, thrashing about.

Gabe hit him again. And again. Until he wasn't moving and Gabe couldn't hear him breathing.

Gabe stood there for a second, chest heaving. Then he dropped the stool. It hit the floor with a clatter.

He raced to Emerson.

She was still sprawled on the floor, one arm raised above her head, her fingers lax. Gabe crouched, his heart pounding harder than it had in the fight. God, she was covered in blood. Her chest and neck were a torn, bloody mess. And the blood... It soaked into her lab coat, turning the normally pristine white crimson.

He leaped up and smacked the emergency alarm button on the wall. They'd been retrofitted along the wall of beds when they'd made this space into the infirmary.

As alarms wailed, he rushed back to Emerson.

"Gabe." She spluttered on the word, blood coming from her mouth.

No. *No.* He got behind her, and gently pulled her head into his lap. "I've got you, Emerson. I'm not letting go. You hold on. Help's coming."

Her hand groped for his and he tangled his fingers with hers.

He couldn't lose her.

But her injury was bad and he knew she was dying. She just had to hold on until they got here. He willed his strength into her.

"You...came."

"Save your strength." He brushed her hair off her face. "And yeah, I came. I can't stay away from you. I'm sorry I was a dick earlier."

Her eyelids fluttered, but her gaze stayed on his. Like looking at him was holding her here.

The doors slammed open and people rushed in. Marcus was in the lead, clutching his carbine. Protocol dictated squad support for the medical staff in an emergency.

Marcus took one look and swore. The medical staff, most in their pajamas, stood gaping in shock.

"Help her!" Gabe yelled.

They rushed forward. An older, black nurse directed them. "Phil, stretcher. Get her into Exam Two."

The woman pressed a hand to the side of Emerson's throat, eyeing the wound with a direct look that steadied Gabe.

"Someone get the nanos prepared. She'll need a

large dose. And blood. She'll need blood. Let's move, people!"

Then the woman's kind brown eyes met Gabe's. "You can let go now. We'll take care of her."

His arms tightened on her, instead.

The woman patted his arm. "Trust me. We love her, too. We'll get her healed."

Gabe sat there and watched them whisk her away. He stayed on the floor, sitting in her blood, remembering one other time he'd been covered in the blood of the one person in the world he loved.

Chapter Nine

"Gabe?"

Marcus' voice pierced the fog that had enveloped Gabe. He had cleaned himself up a little and was sitting on a chair...but his hands were still bloody. Stained with Emerson's blood. Jesus. He felt...hollow.

He looked up at the closed surgery room door. They were still in there. It felt like it had been hours. What if she died? He wouldn't survive.

And all this time he'd held himself back, had been protecting himself and denying them both.

"Gabe," Marcus said again, more sharply.

Gabe turned to look at him. He was standing nearby, his hands on his hips. Gabe had been distantly aware of Marcus directing people to remove the raptor body and store it in the makeshift morgue in the adjoining rooms.

Marcus sat on the chair beside him. "She'll be all right. She's tough."

Gabe wordlessly turned his gaze away from his sergeant and glanced around the room. There were others huddled in small groups across the infirmary, waiting for news. Some were medical staff, and Elle was there with a bunch of civilians. Everybody loved Doc Emerson.

"So, you and the doc?"

Gabe looked over, taken a little aback. Marcus wasn't really one to comment on people's love lives.

Marcus stared at him, then his blue eyes widened the tiniest fraction. "Hell, you're in love with her."

Gabe blinked. Love? He didn't know a lot about love. His father had taken off when he and Zeke were babies, and his mother had not been capable of love. She'd dumped them on their grandmother. Gabe had loved his grandmother. The tough old bird had barely blinked at having two wild young boys to raise. And he'd loved his brother, but they'd never said the word love or talked about it. They'd just always had each other's backs. Had always been there.

Until Zeke hadn't been anymore.

Marcus leaned forward, resting his elbows on his knees. "Loving a woman twists you up. Makes you do some pretty idiotic things. God, it can even make you afraid." He lifted his gaze and Gabe followed it to where Elle was standing, chatting with a nurse. "But it's worth every second."

"What if she doesn't make it?" Gabe finally voiced the words rattling around his head.

"What if she does? What are you going to do then?"

The door opened.

Gabe shot to his feet.

The nurse came out. "She's doing well." Her gaze

skated over the small crowd, before zeroing in on Gabe. "The nanos have healed her wounds. She's a bit shaky and needs some rest."

"I want to see her," Gabe said.

The nurse opened her mouth, and looked like she wanted to deny him. Then she looked at his hands and cleared her throat. "Okay, maybe you'll have better luck convincing her to stay here where someone can keep an eye on her, rather than heading back to her own quarters." The woman shook her head. "Doctors make the worst patients."

Gabe pushed into the room. He half expected to see her flat on her back, but she was sitting up and looked cross. "I hate these gowns," she grumbled.

"Yet you seem to like putting them on others."

She pulled a face. "Doctor's privilege."

"The nurse said you need to stay here and rest."

Emerson shook her head. "No. I'm going to my quarters."

"She said its best—"

"I'm fine, Gabe." Emerson's gaze caught his. "Thank you for rescuing me. If you hadn't arrived when you did—" she shuddered.

And something inside Gabe raged. Like a wild beast yanking at its chain.

"I want my own bed," she continued. "My own things. I'll rest easier and tomorrow I'll be a hundred percent."

He moved closer. Part of him needed to be near her and see that she was truly all right. He looked at her chest, but it was covered by the gown. Her neck, though, looked okay, the new skin a little bit pink from the fresh healing.

"Emerson, you were attacked. You were dying." The word came out strangled. "You have to take it easy."

"And I will. In my quarters."

"We both know you'll drag a tablet and files into bed with you."

She lifted her chin and slid one foot—a slim, rather cute foot with red-painted toenails—to the floor. "You don't get a say in my life, big guy."

He deserved that. He remembered what Reed said about being honest. "Too bad. I'll make sure you rest."

Her mouth dropped open. "You did *not* just say that."

"Yep." He reached down and scooped her into his arms.

She squeaked, snatching at the back of her gown to keep it shut. "Gabe—"

"I agree you'll be more comfortable in your room." He strode out, past the crowd of concerned well-wishers, who all stared at them, wide-eyed. "I'm taking Emerson to her quarters."

The nurse hurried forward and spluttered. "She needs someone to look after her!"

"I'll look after her." He turned and walked out.

Emerson stayed quiet all the way through the tunnels. He waited at her door while she pressed her palm to the lock. The door beeped. Inside, he strode straight to her bed.

"No," she said. "I want to shower first."

He wasn't sure that was a good idea. She had

larger quarters than most, and that included a bathtub. "No. I'll run you a bath." He carried her into the bathroom and set her down on the closed toilet lid and flicked on the water. He pressed the button to close the drain. The water was only lukewarm this time of night. With a frown, he strode out to her kitchenette. It only took him a second to call up some boiling water from the auto-oven. He headed back to the bathroom with the jug. She watched him, bemused.

After a few trips, the water steamed lightly.

"In you hop."

She gripped the medical gown. "After you leave."

He folded his arms over his chest. "I'm not leaving. You might slip, or feel dizzy. I need to be here to help."

She huffed out a breath. "I'm not getting naked in front of you."

His brows rose. "I've seen it all, Emerson." Every glorious inch.

"This is different," she said primly.

He'd never understand women. "Fine. I'm going to get you something to eat. You get in the bath."

"It's the middle of the night. I'm not hungry."

Damn, this looking after someone was hard. "You need the calories after the nano treatment. Now get in the damn bath," he growled.

He was only gone a couple of minutes and returned with some fruit and protein bars.

She was in the tub, the bubbles barely hiding her lush body. In fact, the peek-a-boo show of smooth skin between the white fluff was more arousing than if she'd just been naked. He cursed under his breath, his unruly cock responding.

Jesus, Jackson, she's recovering from an attack.

"I do need to look at my notes, Gabe. Jason...they did something horrible to him." She shuddered. "I'd noticed some strange test results in some of the other lab survivors and after seeing Jason...I know what the Genesis Facility is now." Her eyes were grim. "The aliens are turning humans into raptors."

***

Damn these aliens. Emerson shifted in the bath, the warm water lapping at her skin. The raptors were taking everything, including their humanity.

"Yeah. I guessed as much," Gabe said. "But not tonight. For what's left of the night, you need some sleep."

She swallowed and even though she didn't want to say her next words, she knew they were a necessity. "We need to post guards on the lab survivors. Especially the ones with the abnormal test results."

"Shit. You think some of them could be turning raptor too?"

"I hope not. They've been here a few weeks and I haven't seen any signs of that, but we can't run the risk. Not here in the base."

He rubbed the back of his neck. "Yeah, the raptors have already sent one sleeper spy in here. What's to say there aren't others?"

The thought made her shudder. "The list of the rescued survivors is on my comp and those with the strange results are marked."

"Okay, let me call Marcus." Gabe shot her a hard look. "You eat some of this."

She muttered under her breath as he strode out. But she grabbed a bit of melon. She heard him talking and assumed he'd made the call using her comp.

Soon, he was back. "Marcus said he'd take care of it." Stormy gray eyes hit hers. "And now I'm going to focus on taking care of you."

She felt a flush of heat through her. The nanos had healed her and restored her energy. She wasn't really feeling tired at all.

His gaze dropped to the plate of food. "More." He crouched beside the tub and held up some bite-sized chunks of protein bar.

She groaned. "Gabe. It's the middle of the night."

"More." He wouldn't be budged. "I need to see you eat."

There were nightmares in his eyes.

She heaved out a sigh. "Okay." When she looked again, his gaze had fallen to her bubble-covered breasts. That heat spiked again.

She took her time nibbling strawberries and sucking on melon. Enjoying the laser-focused way he watched her mouth. Finally, she pushed away the rest of the food. "I honestly can't eat anymore."

"Okay." He set the plate on the small vanity. "Lean forward, I'll wash your back."

He grabbed the frothy sponge she had on the

edge of the tub. He squirted her favorite soap on it and sniffed it. "Smells like you." Then he started washing her back. As she leaned forward, he traced along the length of her spine.

"I'm not sure this is a good idea," she murmured. Desire was a slow burn in her belly, but every stroke had it rising higher.

"Need to touch you." Another stroke of the sponge. "Need to feel that you're alive."

God, he was killing her. He worked his way up, kneading her skin a little. She tried to hide a moan, but it escaped her lips.

"I like making you feel good." His hand smoothed over her shoulders, then he lightly circled her throat and put his fingers on her pulse point.

She felt him relax, the air around him losing some intensity.

Her hand came up and touched his. "I'm okay."

"But you weren't." He thumbed that strumming pulse. "You could have died and I..."

He went silent. But Emerson was getting pretty good at reading between the lines with Gabe. The man had no clue how to talk about his feelings. She'd just have to help him. With Gabe, the little gestures and the things he didn't say were most important. "Gabe—"

"I'm done fighting this, Emerson."

She gripped his hand and arched her head back to look at him. "Why were you fighting it?"

"I wanted something better for you."

Better? Better than a brave, tough soldier who

was out there, fighting for everyone else? "I want you."

She felt him shrug. "You know I'm...not like everyone else. I'm dangerous."

"Because of what the army did to you?" She held her breath, waiting to see if he'd finally give her answers.

"I've always been dangerous. From when I was young, I'd walk into the room and note how many people, how big they were and the best way to take them down." He shrugged. "The army just recognized that and made it stronger."

Used him, was more like it. "What did they do?"

"I don't even know everything. Lots of tests, lots of procedures. I know they messed around with my DNA."

She twisted her hands under the water. Just like the raptors were doing to humans now.

"Emerson, I can put my fist through that solid-concrete wall behind you. I can hear the two people walking down the tunnel outside. I can run for three days straight without resting."

She tilted her head. "So?"

He scraped a hand over his head. "Dammit. I could hurt you. One slip and I could be a nightmare."

"I don't believe that."

"And I'm not open and easygoing and loving like you are."

"I know who you are, Gabe." Emerson decided the best way to show him how much she wanted him wasn't with words. She needed him. Now more than ever.

She turned. She knew her breasts were bare to him and his gaze dipped down before coming back to her face.

"Are you finished in there?" he asked. His voice sounded the tiniest bit strangled.

"No. I want you to join me."

His eyes widened just a little. "You were injured," he said slowly.

Emerson decided to bring out the big guns. She cupped her breasts and his chest hitched. "I'm not hurt now."

His fingers gripped the edge of the tub. "My control isn't...great. Seeing you in pain...I don't want to hurt you."

She knew he never would. "How about you come in, sit back and let me do what I want." She nibbled her lip. "I really want to touch you, Gabe."

The moment stretched between them. She knew his answer was important. He'd never let her touch him, explore him.

She could almost see the internal debate going on in his head. Okay, she wasn't above playing dirty. Emerson flicked her nipple, her mouth opening at the spike of pleasure.

Gabe's eyes turned more turbulent. Then he stood and ripped his T-shirt off over his head.

God, he was cut. All those hard ridges of muscle on his stomach, his wide, strong chest. And all that lickable skin.

His hands went to the button and zipper on his jeans. She licked her lips. He stole her breath away, no matter how many times she saw him naked. She was kind of glad that he was a loner and that no other woman in the base had snapped him up.

Hers. He was all hers.

He shucked his trousers and she saw he was already aroused. He stepped into the tub and sat across from her, his long legs on either side of her. Wow, he made the tub seem very, very small.

He didn't say anything, just watched her, need burning in the gray of his eyes.

Yep, all hers. She moved closer and pressed her hands to his chest. He was even harder than she imagined. She traced his hard pecs, learning the shape of them. When she flicked a nail over one flat male nipple, he jerked, water lapping the side of the tub. She looked up. His jaw was clenched. Oh yeah, she was going to have so much fun playing with him.

She took her time. She explored his chest, his hard biceps. He had a tattoo across his chest. Some writing done in a coiling, elegant script. She made out Ezekiel and the name Gramma. "Zeke and I both had them. He had my name and our grandmother's. She raised us. She deserved so much more than this—" he traced the tattoo "—but it was all we had to give her at the time. We were fifteen."

"A little young to get a tattoo."

"We snuck into a tattoo place. Because we were both so big, they bought our story of being eighteen."

"Your parents?"

"Never knew whoever fathered us. Our mother wasn't worth the title. Dumped us on Gramma and took off. Popped in occasionally. Called to wish us happy birthday...when it wasn't our birthday."

Emerson smoothed her fingers over his tattoo. "I like it."

She kept stroking him. His skin was a dark, gleaming bronze that she loved. The doctor in her appreciated a healthy male who kept himself in such good shape. The woman in her appreciated it even more.

A big hand reached out and cupped her breast. She looked at his hand, so large yet gentle on her skin. As he caressed her, her eyes fluttered closed. *So good.*

She let her hands drift lower and cup his cock. Big and hard. She already knew the pleasure he could bring her, but now it was her chance to drive him to madness. To see him shed some of that control he held onto too tightly.

She shifted onto his lap, straddling his hips. His other hand cupped her other breast.

Emerson kissed him. She loved the smoky flavor of his mouth. He tried to take over the kiss, but she stroked her tongue against his and let him know she was with him every step of this dance.

Then she circled his cock again, gave it one hard stroke and lifted her hips up. She lined the thick head up between her legs and sank down.

Their joint groans echoed in the small bathroom. Emerson couldn't go slowly. She lifted up, sliding off him, then down. God, he stretched her. Filled her up. She started riding him, his hands digging into her hips.

"Emerson," he groaned.

She moved faster, harder, taking him deeper. His gaze was on hers, burning hot.

She wanted this feeling of being one to last forever. Dimly, she heard water spilling out of the bath onto the tiles but she didn't care.

His hand slipped between her thighs, and he found her clit. She kept riding him, felt the hard pressure of his thumb on her slick nub.

She felt her orgasm growing, threatening with every tightening muscle in her body.

He started slamming her down hard, groans escaping his chest.

Release hit like a blinding explosion. Emerson heard herself scream, the sound echoing around them. Gabe thrust her down once more, hard, and his own hoarse shout joined hers.

As he spilled inside her, she collapsed against his chest. His heartbeat was a rapid beat beneath her ear. Alive. They were both alive and for now, that was all that mattered.

Chapter Ten

Gabe hadn't felt this content since...well, ever.

He and Emerson sat on her couch. He was sipping his morning coffee, and she was snuggled against his side. She held a glass of juice in one hand and was wearing only his T-shirt. They'd just finished the breakfast he'd made. Gabe actually didn't mind cooking, but he'd never had a good enough reason to make the effort. He breathed deep, inhaling her scent. Now he did.

A lot of the food was still on the table. Maybe he'd gone a little overboard—toast, substitute eggs, pancakes. She'd groaned and pleaded that she was full.

She looked good today. Rested, a touch of color in her cheeks, and satisfaction in her eyes.

He could stay sitting here with her for a very long time.

There was a knock at the door.

Emerson sat up, and Gabe scowled. "I'll get it."

He opened the door. To the members of Hell Squad.

"Hey, man," Shaw breezed in. "We wanted to check on the doc."

Claudia sauntered in behind the sniper. "He just wants freshly cooked food."

"How's Emerson?" Reed asked.

"Better," Gabe growled.

"Good to hear." Cruz moved in, too, followed by a smiling Santha. They headed to where the others were picking at the breakfast leftovers.

Marcus raised a brow. "We also need to talk about what happened last night."

Gabe nodded. Apparently, their quiet morning was over. After Marcus stepped inside, Gabe closed the door. Emerson's quarters felt a lot smaller with the squad lounging around everywhere. Claudia hitched herself onto the kitchen bench, eating a slice of toast. Shaw sat at the table scarfing food. Reed, Cruz, and Santha leaned against the far wall, all of them with mugs of coffee. Marcus sat in an armchair near the couch.

Emerson was blinking, staring at them with a slightly bemused expression. She was probably used to loads of people...in the infirmary. Not in her private space. Especially a rough crowd like these guys.

Plus, she was only wearing his shirt, which left her shapely legs on display for everyone to see. He hurried over and sat back down, hauling her to his side.

Claudia raised a brow. "So, you guys finally going public?"

He felt Emerson tense beside him, waiting for his response. Gabe expected the question to leave him anxious. He waited. Nope. He didn't feel

104

anything except savage satisfaction. He wanted to stake his claim on Emerson and make sure everyone knew she was his.

When he stayed relaxed, Emerson relaxed too, melting against him. She looked up. "Big guy?"

"Hell, yeah," he said.

Claudia smiled.

Shaw sat back in his chair, grinning. "Good job, man. The doc is smart as hell, pretty as hell and sexy as hell."

Emerson choked on a laugh. "I'm sitting right here, Shaw."

His grin was unrepentant. "So? I'm just telling you like it is."

Claudia shook her head. "Ignore him. I think he was missing brain cells at birth."

Shaw shot her the finger before snatching up a protein-substitute sausage.

Marcus leaned forward in his chair, his expression shifting from faintly amused to serious. "We need to talk about Jason."

"I've been collecting data from the lab survivors," Emerson said. "Doing tests, trying to work out what the raptors did to them and why. Most of it was confusing, and made no sense." She drew a deep breath. "But after seeing what they did to poor Jason...there's obviously only one conclusion. The aliens are turning humans into raptors."

There was a round of swearing.

"How the hell can they do that?" Reed asked.

"They're messing with human DNA. I don't

know yet, can only speculate. I'd guess they are somehow injecting raptor DNA into humans. The strange thing is, I haven't been able to isolate raptor DNA. We've had the prisoner downstairs in the cells and I've taken live samples, as well as some from the corpses I've studied. Their DNA is either too complex, or something else is going on. It's like each one of them has different DNA."

There was an unhappy silence.

"So, this Genesis Facility and these tanks, it's for changing people into aliens?" Gabe asked.

Emerson nodded. "The three tanks we saw at Luna Park lab, those people couldn't have been in there very long. They weren't showing any raptor attributes."

"I saw some of them had darkened patches of skin," Santha said.

Emerson nodded. "They were just at the beginning of the change."

Santha's face twisted. "When I fought the commander—"

Gabe felt Emerson tense, no doubt thinking of her captivity. He pulled her closer and she pressed a hand over his heart.

"The commander said they were here to make our species stronger. I thought she wanted us to join them."

Emerson sucked in a breath. "You think they're actually here for humans? As a...resource to create more of their raptor soldiers?"

"Yes."

Cruz stirred. "But they've killed so many people."

It was Marcus who answered. "They couldn't have controlled the entire planet's population."

Gabe nodded. "Thin us out to a manageable level. Start changing those you capture..."

Emerson bolted upright. "And keep hunting down any survivors who are left." Her gaze caught Gabe's.

He cupped her cheek. "No fucking alien is going to turn you into a raptor."

Silence fell, everyone thinking.

Gabe looked at the others. He realized over the last year, they'd become his family. They'd had his back, called him out when he was an idiot. He'd thought when Zeke had died that he'd lost everything. Yet here he was, his arms around his woman, and both of them surrounded by his brothers-at-arms.

"We have to destroy the Genesis Facility," he said.

"And get word out to any other human bases to look out for this," Emerson added. "Who knows how many Genesis Facilities there are across the planet?"

"Surely making those tanks takes time," Shaw added. "Destroying them would have to set them back."

The sniper hid his very alert mind behind a lazy, good-ol'-boy charm. But Gabe had fought alongside the guy long enough to know he was as sharp as a combat knife. "Yeah, but even if we destroy this facility, we're still only nipping at them. Taking tiny little bites." It wasn't enough.

Cruz stepped forward. "Remember what Santha said to the commander before she killed her?"

Santha groaned. "Not my speech again."

Cruz stroked a hand down her arm. "We keep nipping. We keep slicing. They'll bleed out eventually."

Gabe nodded, but what if humanity couldn't last that long? His hands tightened on Emerson. What if before the aliens lost enough blood to weaken them, they turned all the remaining humans into fucking raptors?

"My team is still looking for the Genesis Facility." Santha looked frustrated. "But I won't lie. We've covered most of the raptor's main territory. I'm not sure it's in the city, or if it is, they are hiding it too well."

Emerson set her legs on the floor, tugging on the hem of her shirt. "Well, I'm going to start by autopsying Jas—" she grimaced. "—the raptor-human hybrid. See what else I can find out."

Gabe stood. "I'm coming with you."

"I'll be fine."

"But I'm not." Okay, he felt the tiniest bit weird admitting that. But it was the truth. He saw Reed smile and nod at him. Gabe looked at Emerson. "I want to be there."

Her lips twitched. "Okay." Then her face turned serious. "After that, I need to examine all the raptor lab survivors."

Cruz cursed and Santha grabbed his hand. They

were no doubt thinking of Bryony.

"The last thing we need," Marcus said, "is for others to also turn into raptors."

"Like sleeper agents," Gabe added.

Emerson nodded. "I hope not, but it's a possibility. We need to be sure."

Gabe's jaw tightened. Those poor people had already been through so much.

***

Emerson slipped on her protective goggles. She looked down at Jason's body laid out on the metal autopsy table. "Poor guy."

Gabe grunted from where he stood at the side of the small autopsy room, his arms crossed over his chest.

She circled the table to her tray of tools. "He didn't ask for what was done to him, Gabe. I feel sorry for him."

"He hurt you. I can't forgive that."

Her heart bumped around in her chest. Damn, she'd never thought alpha male attitude would do it for her.

She reached for her saw, but Gabe stepped closer. "Before you start, I have something for you." He pulled an item from his pocket. "I meant to give it to you earlier, but…"

Right. She'd been attacked by an alien-human hybrid.

He held out a brand new m-scanner.

She gasped. It was a newer model than hers,

with extra functionality she'd dreamed about a hundred times.

She stroked the sleek piece of equipment. "Where did you get this?"

"Came across it out in the field."

Yeah, right. He'd just happened to pass by a brand-new m-scanner while out on a mission. Her chest warmed. He'd gotten it for her. She took it. "It's wonderful, Gabe. Thank you."

He shrugged. "It's not like it's diamonds, or anything."

"No." She turned the scanner over. "But I'm not really a diamonds kind of gal." She gripped his broad shoulders and went up on tip toe to kiss him.

She'd intended for it to be a quick thank-you kiss, but his arms wrapped around her and yanked her against his chest. He deepened the kiss until she pulled back, gasping for air.

"I have work," she said, voice breathy.

With a nod, he traced a finger over her lips. His gray eyes glowed.

"What are you feeling right now?" she asked.

He thought for a second. "Satisfaction. Happiness."

He was learning. She smiled and shooed him away. He moved back to his spot by the wall.

Emerson took a few calming breaths. The man destroyed her equilibrium. Then she turned to her unpleasant task.

Once she started the examination, Emerson lost herself in her work. She'd become a doctor to help people but she'd always had a fascination with the

110

human body. How everything fit together, how it all worked. While other little girls were dressing as princesses and reading fairytales, Emerson had a dress-up lab coat and begged her parents for anatomy books.

When she opened Jason up, she was shocked by what she found. Alien tissue riddled his insides. Some of his organs even looked different, enlarged with growths on them. Stringy fiber stretched through his chest cavity and surrounded his heart. Vein-like tubes carried an orange fluid that glowed. She shook her head. It was going to take her a long time to sort through this.

She dictated notes to her comp, removed organs and weighed them. When she lifted her head and stretched her neck, she saw Gabe was still standing in the same place. "You're still here? God, Gabe you should have gone and grabbed some lunch. How long have I been at it?" She glanced at the clock on the wall.

"Three hours," he said. "It's not a problem. There have been loads of missions I've had to wait longer than this. Besides, I could watch you work all day. All that competence."

She glanced at her gloved hand clutching the saw. All of it covered in blood. "I've been autopsying a dead half-alien body."

"Could still watch you all day."

She shook her head, but smiled.

"You find anything important?"

"Well, there's a lot of alien in him. I'd guess the transition takes time and he's been with them several months." Maybe floating in one of those genesis tanks. Then she studied the glowing orange fluid again. "There's this strange fluid everywhere. We know raptor blood is red like ours, but this orange stuff..."

"Lymph?" Gabe suggested.

"I don't think so. I think it might be a part of the transformation process." She'd already taken some samples to run through the analyzer. She also lifted her new scanner and ran it over the fluid. "Completely alien. The scanner can't even isolate everything it's made of. I'll have to run some manual tests." She paused. "It has a really unique signature...and it's very easy to pick up on the scanners."

Gabe straightened. "You saying we can scan for it?"

Emerson tried to tamp down the surge of excitement. "Maybe."

"Send everything you have on it to Elle and Santha. They can see what we can do."

Emerson nodded. It took another hour to finish up with Jason. She said a quiet farewell as she bagged his body and set it in the morgue storage. They'd have to keep his remains for further testing. She hoped he was in a better place now.

After she'd cleaned up, Gabe motioned her out the door. "We'll grab some sandwiches, then head over to Ops. Santha says they already have drones up scanning for the fluid."

Emerson blinked. "That fast?"

"They roped Noah into helping. He rigged a few

drones and got them in the air. Says he can do more if we need them."

They hurried through the tunnels and, after a quick stop in the dining room, reached Ops. As they walked through the Hive, General Holmes stepped in front of them.

"Emerson? You're doing okay?"

"Yes, General." Emerson liked the leader of Blue Mountain Base. He was always calm and steadfast in the face of any crisis. He'd single-handedly created the squads, and got the base into some sort of order, organizing medical, research, tech, schooling, food stores. Not to mention teams to protect the base.

Without him, she guessed a lot more survivors would have died and they'd all be a lot more uncomfortable. She knew he often clashed with the squad leaders, but he had to weigh up the benefits to all, not just a few, and that meant he couldn't be popular. It was a tough job. She'd seen him once or twice for private medical checkups. He was under a great deal of stress, which he never allowed anyone to see. Emerson worried if he didn't find something to relieve the stress, to help him bear the load, it might swallow him up.

"Jackson, I hear you saved the doctor. Good work."

Gabe nodded. "Yes, sir."

"Elle also tells me you might have found a way to scan for the Genesis Facility?" He fell into step beside them.

"We hope so," Emerson replied. "We have to see

if it'll work, first."

"It's a start. That's all we need."

Chapter Eleven

Gabe watched as Santha directed one of the drone operators, a redheaded woman named Lia. The footage on the large main screen in the Hive showed a drone flying over the shattered ruins of the skyscrapers in the city center.

Behind him, the rest of Hell Squad stood, watching in silence.

"So far, nothing," Santha said over her shoulder.

"You're sure this scanner you rigged up will work?" Gabe asked.

Noah Kim stirred in his chair. "I don't ask you if you can take down a raptor or fire your carbine."

Sitting beside the tech guru, Elle looked like she was trying not to laugh. "The scanner will work, but Lia has to fly the drone low to pick up the fluid signature."

The redhead didn't take her eyes off the screen. "Exactly. There's a greater chance I'll hit something." She moved her hands through the air in a hypnotic dance. She was wearing a set of thin, black gloves with glowing wires running through them.

"She's flying it manually?" Emerson asked. "I thought the drones flew themselves."

Noah nodded. "They do. And when there aren't too many obstacles the programming works well. But with more to run into and a more complex task, you can't beat manual. As long as the operator knows what they're doing."

Gabe thought Lia looked more than competent.

The woman in question cast a quick look back. Large almond-shaped eyes dominated her face. "And I certainly know what I'm doing, Kim."

"What did you do before, Lia?" Emerson asked.

"Commercial pilot," the woman answered.

The comp made a pinging noise. Everyone straightened, the air in the room going taut.

Lia tapped at the comp screen, then she looked back and grinned. "We've picked something up west of the city center. Going in for a closer look."

Images filled the screen. Elle frowned. "It's a sports stadium. Is that where the signal's coming from?"

Lia nodded. "It's Stadium Australia. A multi-purpose stadium that's been renovated and rebuilt numerous times over the years. It was first built for the Olympics."

Gabe eyed the decaying ruin of the stadium. From a distance, it looked almost normal. Like a sports team could head in there and play a game at any moment.

But as the drone got closer, it was easy to see that one side of the complex was damaged. The wall had been smashed through. A rampaging rex, Gabe decided. He had a strong dislike for the giant creatures.

Elle was tapping another comp screen. "I'm picking up raptor signatures." Her mouth tightened. "Not a lot of them, but they are getting better at hiding from the drone scans."

Noah tapped his fingers against the table in front of him. "I'm working on that."

"Good. I hate seeing the squads go in without the right intel." The comms officer's gaze went to Marcus.

"Okay, definite readings for this alien goo," Lia said.

"Look." Santha pointed.

Gabe leaned forward, the rest of the squad doing the same. At first, he didn't see anything. Wait...now he saw them moving out of the stadium. God, Santha had good eyes.

A small group of raptor soldiers were walking, keeping an unarmed raptor between them. As the drone camera zoomed in, the middle raptor glanced around and was talking. Probably issuing orders, as two soldiers peeled off.

Then the lead raptor looked up. Like he was looking directly at the drone.

One red eye, the other covered in a nasty, ugly scar.

Gabe's hands curled into fists and he heard Emerson gasp. Her hand groped for his and she squeezed it.

"Hello, One Eye," Shaw murmured.

Gabe looked over at Marcus. "Hell Squad going in?"

"Yeah." Marcus' face was turned toward the screen.

Gabe didn't say anything else. Marcus would know what he was asking.

Hell Squad's leader turned his head. "You keep it together, you're back in the field."

Good. Gabe nodded.

"All right, Hell Squad. You know the drill."

Gabe gave Emerson a quick kiss.

"Be careful," she said.

He stayed silent. He couldn't promise that. He'd try, but he wouldn't lie to her. He'd do whatever needed to be done.

She sighed and pressed her palms to his chest. "Come back to me, okay, big guy?" She pressed her lips to his, a fleeting touch.

He wanted more. But it wasn't the time. With a nod, he followed the team.

In the squad locker room, he put his armor on and checked his carbine. A deadly calm settled over him. Destroy the raptors' shit and kill this one-eyed raptor. If he could do that, he could finally be rid of the darkness inside. Be a better man for Emerson.

He looked up and saw Marcus watching him.

"We end this," Marcus said.

"Yeah." Gabe would. For the brother he'd lost, for the woman he'd been gifted with.

"Remember, we're a team. I don't have to remind you what got you sidelined last time."

Gabe's jaw tightened. "I got it."

"All right. Let's get on the Hawk. We're heading out to pick up the Hunters."

"We're driving in?" Gabe asked.

"Yeah. You might have missed the way that raptor fucking looked right at the drone, but I didn't."

"I saw. He couldn't have known it was there, could he?"

"Not taking the risk. They won't expect us to come in on wheels."

Around them, the squad finished getting ready—slipping combat knives into sheaths, slinging carbines over their shoulders. They made their way to the landing pads.

The Hawk was waiting for them, rotors already spinning.

The team climbed aboard. Marcus slammed the side door closed and called out to Finn. As the Hawk lifted off, Gabe spotted Emerson watching them leave. For the first time, he felt the burning need to get the mission done and get back to her. He watched her until he couldn't see her anymore.

The Hawk flew over trees, a few smaller towns. It was a dull, dreary day, the sky packed with gray clouds. Finally, they flew over a dilapidated, abandoned area that looked like it had once been a farm.

Except Gabe knew it was no farm.

Unlike the last time they'd come here, they didn't land near the ruined sheds. Instead, Finn set them down in a clearing amongst the trees. They never used the same entrance to the Hunter facility more than twice in a row.

Marcus leaped off the Hawk and the rest of

them followed. They had their carbines in their hands, but not aimed. Raptors didn't like trees. Marcus led them to a large area of rocks. He moved to one, uncovered a hidden keypad and tapped in a code. A cleverly hidden door disguised as rocks slid open. He waved them in.

The narrow tunnel ran straight for a bit before descending. They all clicked on the tactical flashlights attached to their carbines. Soon, they reached a door and stepped into an underground parking facility.

The Z6-Hunters were parked in a row. The experimental vehicles were black, armor-plated personnel carriers with autocannons mounted on top. They had a few more dings and scratches now than they'd had a year ago.

"All right. Gabe and Claudia, you're with me. Cruz, Reed and Shaw, take the second vehicle."

Everyone did as ordered. Gabe raised a brow at Claudia. She waved at the slightly elevated autocannon seat. "You take it."

Hell, yeah. He climbed up and settled into the seat. The autocannon's controls and virtual heads-up display flashed to life in front of him. He fitted his hands around the autocannon controls, and prayed he got to use it. They had an automatic setting and could target and fire themselves, but it was much more fun on manual.

Soon Marcus was pulling the Hunter up the exit ramp, Cruz's Hunter following close behind.

Elle's voice came through their earpieces. "I've mapped out the best route to the stadium. There are raptor patrols in the air, so I'll let you know if any get too close. Illusion systems up?"

"Yeah." Marcus's gravelly reply.

"You got it, Ellie," Cruz confirmed.

The illusion system was an awesome piece of tech that, while didn't cloak the Hunters completely, did the next best thing. It blurred them, messed with their signatures on raptor scans, and used directed sound waves to distort any noise and make the enemy think they were in a different location. The Hawks had them too.

The journey through the ruined suburbs, past empty schools and looted shops, was uneventful.

As they neared the stadium, Gabe saw its distinctive shape ahead in the distance.

"I'm not picking up any raptor signatures," Elle said, a frown evident in her voice. "Not one."

"You still picking up the alien substance?" Marcus asked.

"Yes."

"Then they can't be far away."

Gabe searched the area, but didn't see anything. Nothing was moving out there.

"Wait!" Elle's frantic voice came through loud and clear. "I got a flicker of something. Wait a second...oh, God, Marcus you have three...no, *four* raptor ground vehicles inbound."

A second after she said it, Gabe saw them. Everyone else cursed, but Gabe calmly swung the autocannon around. The raptor vehicles were squat and ugly, with large spikes sticking out at the front. He's always thought they'd resembled some dinosaur, a triceratops maybe. He knew the armor plating was tough as hell.

But not tough enough for an autocannon.

He opened fire, the deadly green laser cutting through the gloomy afternoon.

A second later, Shaw did the same from the second Hunter.

The four black vehicles split apart.

"Marcus! Swing us round," Gabe yelled, twisting the autocannon as far as he could. Laser cut across the hull of the passing raptor vehicle, scoring the side of it.

The vehicles roared around them. Marcus gunned the Hunter, glancing at his rear camera view. Gabe touched his display and the camera image flashed up.

The raptor vehicles were coming back.

"Cruz," Marcus said. "Let's pull that maneuver we used back in Syria with the Hummers."

"Good idea, *amigo*."

When the raptors returned, Marcus and Cruz yanked the wheels and the Hunters veered left.

"Gabe, Shaw, keep the others off us. And everyone, hold on."

A second later, Cruz pulled in an inch behind their Hunter. And a second after that, Marcus and Cruz rammed the Hunters into the isolated raptor vehicle.

Ahead, water shimmered. Homebush Bay was a dull, dark gray, reflecting the lack of sun and sullen clouds.

Another ram by the two Hunters and the alien

vehicle lost control. It zigged and zagged, before running straight into the harbor, landing with a giant splash.

"Woo-hoo!" Shaw yelled. "Now spin us around, Cruz. I got some shooting to do. Gabe, let's hit the same one and even the odds."

"The one on the far left?"

"Got it."

Together they targeted their cannon fire. Marcus and Cruz drove to give them a perfect view of their prey.

Flames and smoke appeared from the back of the vehicle. A moment later, the raptor vehicle hit a parked car, flipped and crashed down.

"Two down, two to go," Marcus said.

But the other two vehicles were wary, keeping their distance.

Soon, the Hunters and the two alien vehicles were racing down the streets. The hulking form of the stadium was close now.

They roared into a large, empty parking lot.

The raptor vehicles did some fancy maneuvers. But Marcus and Cruz kept on them.

And this time, the raptors were returning fire. Deadly raptor poison arced through the air.

"Fuck." Marcus swerved to avoid being hit, but a small splatter caught the rear of the Hunter.

Burning metal sizzled, and the ugly, smoky smell caught Gabe's nose. He glanced back—right through a small hole the raptor poison had chewed through the vehicle.

"Gabe?"

"It's okay. Minor damage."

Suddenly, Marcus braked. The Hunter skidded and he swung the vehicle around. Gabe sighted the next raptor vehicle and fired the autocannon. The alien vehicle lost control and hit a pile of rubble. It exploded in a giant ball of flames.

"Woot!" Shaw called out. "Last one's mine, Jackson. Hands off."

Thirty seconds later, the final raptor vehicle—already scorched by laser fire—crashed into the side of the stadium.

Hell Squad pulled to a stop. As they climbed out, Gabe eyed the horizon. The sky had begun to dim, and he thought of base, of Emerson.

"It'll be dark soon," he said.

"Yeah." Marcus didn't sound happy.

Night was always problematic in the city. And lately, the few survivors making it to Blue Mountain Base also talked about strange attacks in the dark that left people a bloody mass of meat.

"Come on," Marcus said. "Hell Squad, ready to go to Hell?"

"Hell, yeah! The devil needs an ass-kicking!"

Cautiously, guns up, they moved into the tunnel leading into the stadium. Their boots made a faint echo on the cement, but the place was empty. As they stepped out into the stadium itself, at the base of the rows and rows of empty seats, Gabe felt a flash of sorrow. This place had once been full of life, with people laughing, celebrating, and cheering on their favorite athletes.

Now it was an empty relic, mocking the past.

He shook his head to clear the gloomy thoughts. Kill raptors. That was all he should be thinking about.

They walked along a row of seats.

"Gabe, you see anything?"

He had better vision than the others, but didn't spot anything unusual in the growing shadows. "Negative."

"All right, let's switch to night vision."

Gabe flicked the lens across his right eye. Instantly, everything around him appeared in shades of green.

"I really, really don't like this," Shaw said.

They stepped out on the central field of the stadium. The grass was the same high-tech turf that most stadiums had switched to years ago. It was made of recycled products and it was virtually impossible to tell it apart from real grass. But Gabe could tell now. Instead of being brown and crunchy from lack of care and water, it was still a vibrant, unrealistic green.

Hell Squad moved as a group, quiet and tense. Still nothing. Overhead, clouds formed a dark, roiling mass that blanketed the sky.

Shaw was looking up. Through the high-tech scope of his long range laser rifle. Gabe followed his gaze.

One strange cloud was larger, and blacker, than the others. And it was moving, twisting.

"What the fuck?" Shaw said.

Everyone turned, looked up.

"What is it?" Marcus demanded.

"No idea." Shaw shook his head. "I can't make it out."

Gabe kept staring. The cloud was growing larger.

And heading toward them.

His pulse tripped. "It's a mass of some sort of animals! Birds, maybe."

"Shit. Get to cover," Marcus roared.

They started running, but they were only half-way across the field when the swarm hit.

Chapter Twelve

Sharp things nipped and slashed and bit at Gabe. *Fuck*.

He heard the rest of the squad cursing and yelling. It was like a cloud of bats. Gabe pulled one arm over his head, batting at the creatures with his other hand.

One animal landed on the grass at his feet. Not a bat. A tiny, winged, dinosaur-like alien with barbed wings, sharp teeth, and curved claws.

He heard some of Hell Squad shooting. Gabe swung his carbine around. They were too small to shoot at, but maybe they could scare them off. If they could see them in the growing darkness. He flicked on his tactical flashlight.

With a high-pitched squeal, the creatures rushed away from him in a flutter of wings. He frowned, then he realized. "The light! They don't like the light."

The others flicked their flashlights on. It left them in a small cocoon of safety. At the edge of the light, the aliens screamed and flapped their wings. The team kept moving and Gabe glanced around. Everyone was bleeding, faces covered in cuts and blood. Reed had a hand over one eye, blood oozing between his fingers.

Then Gabe looked up. Oh, no. "Hellions!"

The canid-like creatures were pouring down the sides of the stadium, leaping over seats and railings. Their bellies glowed red, filled with acidic poison.

"Use your cedar-oil grenades," Marcus yelled.

Gabe snatched his off his belt. Santha had come up with the substance and canids and hellions hated the stuff.

He tossed his canister. He heard the bang and the hiss of spray. Around him, the others were doing the same.

"Won't hold them for long," Marcus yelled. "Elle, we're pinned down. Everyone's got minor injuries. We need to retreat."

Retreat? Gabe's stomach clenched. No, they had to find the head raptor and the Genesis tanks. "But we're so goddamned close."

Marcus' eyes gleamed in the shadows. "We won't give up. But we won't die for it, either."

Gabe gritted his teeth and looked again at Reed. The guy had moved his hand and was probing his cheekbone. His eye was a bloody, gouged mess. Gabe cursed. The sensible thing to do was retreat.

But that dark, angry part of him didn't want to turn back.

"Hellions are almost here," Shaw said. He was firing, picking off what alien dogs he could. The others were braced and ready, guns up. Claudia looked like she'd gone head-to-head with a serial killer and lost. Her face was covered in ugly scratches and cuts. And right now, you couldn't tell Cruz had a face the ladies at base drooled over.

"Marcus," Elle said. "There's a tunnel exit into the team locker rooms. To the east."

Marcus turned. "Got it. Hell Squad, let's get back to the Hunters. Pull in and stay close."

They entered the narrow tunnel. The hellions were yowling and yipping outside. The squad was walking backwards, guns aimed.

They did not want to get caught in this tunnel with the hellions.

The first creature bounded in through the tunnel entrance. The team opened fire, the sound of their carbines deafening in the enclosed space. They kept up the steady stream of laser fire and kept moving backward.

One hellion managed to get through. Gabe yanked out his combat knife and leaped forward to meet it. Adrenaline roared through his blood stream. He kicked the animal in its tooth-filled mouth and stabbed it in the neck, avoiding its poisonous belly.

As the alien dropped down dead, he kicked it away and swung his carbine back up.

"Left!" Marcus roared.

Gabe looked. The tunnel had opened up into locker rooms. He spotted an emergency exit light, still lit. No doubt powered by some tiny nuclear reactor still running in the bowels of the stadium.

The squad moved through the locker room. Cruz slammed the door to the tunnel shut. "Help me with some of these lockers."

Shaw and Gabe helped him manhandle some of the metal lockers in place. A second later, weight hit the other side of the door, making the door and the lockers shudder.

"Let's keep moving." Marcus headed out through the opposite doors.

They passed offices, shower rooms, medical treatment rooms.

Elle's voice came again. "At the end of the corridor you'll find stairs leading up. They'll bring you to the main level and you can get out to the parking lot."

"Roger that, Elle." Marcus gestured them on. "Reed? You okay?"

Reed's face screwed up. "I can't see much. This eye is messed up and the other's got blood in it."

"Claudia, stay near Reed."

"You need Claudia bringing up the rear, not babysitting me—"

"Your vision is compromised. Gabe, watch our ass. Now, let's get the fuck out of here."

They rounded a corner. Ahead, Gabe saw the stairs, and everyone moved steadily towards them.

A noise behind him made him turn.

He stiffened. The one-eyed raptor stood in a nearby doorway.

And he was holding Emerson in front of him, an ugly, scaled hand clenching a gun that was jammed up under her chin.

Gage lifted his carbine, his heart roaring in his ears. "Marcus!"

Marcus cursed. Emerson made a small sobbing sound.

Gabe blinked. Not Emerson. Another woman who looked similar, with her blonde hair gleaming in the darkness.

The raptor stared at Gabe with his glowing red eye, then stepped backward out of view, dragging the woman with him.

Gabe took a step forward. One shot. That was all he needed. One good shot and he could end the fucker and rescue that woman. He took another step toward the doorway.

"Gabe!" Marcus growled. "We have to go. Reed's injured, we can't—"

"He's got a woman, Marcus." A woman who looked like Emerson. It would only take a second.

He strode through the doorway. It was a large, open-plan office area. Empty except for now-dusty desks. Across the room, another door stood open.

"Gabe?" Marcus' furious whisper across the comms. "Where the fuck are you?"

"I'm in pursuit."

"No, dammit!"

Suddenly gunfire ripped across the comms. Marcus was bellowing orders, the others were yelling. The squad was under attack.

Gabe turned, he had to get back. Then the raptor appeared, the woman still in front of him.

Gabe fired. The shot was high, he couldn't risk hitting the woman. The raptor dodged it easily.

"I'll get you out of here," Gabe yelled.

The woman lifted her head. And laughed.

Gabe tensed. Her eyes were glowing a faint red and her face was covered in patches of scales.

Fuck. The bastard had lured him in here...and like an idiot, he'd followed.

"Grenade," Cruz shouted.

Gabe heard the violent bang. Heard one of the team yell in pain.

The raptor said something in his guttural language. Three huge hellions slunk into the room behind him.

And it was then Gabe saw the clear boxes stacked by the wall. All filled with an orange fluid.

A trap. It had all been one giant trap.

Another guttural word from One Eye and the hellions launched at Gabe.

He shot the first right through the eye. The other two were leaping at him in a flash. Gabe yanked out his knife and a second later, the creatures' weight hit him, driving him to the ground.

They seemed to know all the weakest spots in his armor. They ripped and clawed at him, jaws snapping. He felt a lash of fire, smelled his own blood. The damned things were no mindless beasts. They were learning.

"Another grenade!" Someone shouted.

Another boom outside in the hall.

"Fuck, Reed is down. Reed is down. Cruz, get him." Marcus' voice was strained.

Gabe was in hell. He fought to keep the hellions' jaws away from his face. His squad was injured.

He wondered if this was it. If this was the day

that Hell Squad finally lost. They'd never find the Genesis Facility. And Gabe would finally die at the claws of the raptors.

Then he thought of Emerson.

Fuck no. She was waiting, and his team needed him.

With a giant heave, he rolled. Using all his enhanced strength, he slammed his knife into the mouth of the nearest hellion. Its teeth raked along his armor, but he finally hit something and blood gushed out of the animal's mouth. Gabe swung around and slammed the blade into the second hellion as it poised to strike. He hit tough scales, but he used his legs, putting everything he had into working the knife deeper.

The hellion made a horrible keening cry and flopped to the floor.

Gabe staggered to his feet, a little lightheaded. The raptor and the hybrid woman were gone.

He rushed out into the hall. He skidded to a stop, his chest tightening.

The corridor was filled with dead raptor and hellion bodies.

At the far end, near the stairs, Marcus was on his knees. He was coated in blood and gore, his chest heaving. Claudia was sprawled on the ground to one side, her dark braid stark against the white tiles that were smeared with blood. Shaw wrapped around her and—bile rose in Gabe's throat—the back of the sniper's armor was torn open and pitted with shrapnel. He'd clearly taken the brunt of the grenade blast.

On the other side of the corridor, Reed and Cruz were lying in heaps against the wall, where the blast had obviously thrown them. Neither were moving.

Gabe ran forward. He had to get them out of here.

"Marcus?"

The other man blinked slowly, his eyes unfocused. Gabe then noticed a piece of shrapnel lodged in his leader's head. *Damn.*

"Come on." Gabe heaved Marcus up. "I need you to carry Claudia. Can you do it?"

Marcus turned to look where she lay and nodded.

"Okay." Gabe yanked a field iono-stretcher off his belt. It took him three seconds to open and activate it. It hovered off the ground, using electrohydrodynamics to produce the thrust to stay in the air. He quickly picked up Reed and laid him on the stretcher. Then he hefted Cruz over one shoulder and clumsily managed to get Shaw over the other. The exoskeleton in Gabe's armor helped take most of the men's weight, and his enhanced strength helped, too. Still, it was awkward and left him unable to shoot well.

"Let's go."

Marcus weaved up the steps, Claudia clutched in his arms. Gabe nudged the stretcher and it floated up. They made it to the top and Gabe directed Marcus to the main entrance.

Gabe paused at the doorway. Outside, the night was dark. He didn't want to risk those bat-like aliens attacking again.

In the parking lot, he scanned all the accumulated trash that had built up. It looked like someone had made a small camp there at one stage. He spied an old propane tank.

Please still have something inside. He turned a little and aimed his carbine. The sustained burst of laser hit the tank and a few seconds later, it exploded. It bathed an area of the parking lot with light.

"Go. Stick to the light. Get to the Hunters."

They ambled across the lot. Gabe kept praying no more hellions or raptors poured out after them.

The Hunters appeared out of the darkness. A very welcome sight.

Gabe dumped Cruz on the ground beside the vehicle. He loaded Shaw in the back, then Reed, and finally Cruz. Their second-in-command stirred a little, but the others were so silent it made Gabe's gut cramp.

Next, he helped Marcus get Claudia in the front.

"Can't lose a Hunter," Marcus said.

Shit. Gabe eyed the second vehicle. It would be a blow. It was impossible to replace, but Marcus was in no shape to drive it.

"Get in beside Claudia. I'll take care of it." Gabe touched his earpiece. "Elle?"

"How are they doing?" she asked anxiously.

"They need Emerson. Look, I've got them loaded in a Hunter. I'm bringing them home."

Elle released a shaky sigh. "Good. Okay."

"No one's well enough to drive the other

Hunter."

"Oh, no."

"But I have an idea. Can you patch Lia into the vehicle's systems?"

Elle was quiet a second. "Yes. You want her to remotely operate it? It's not like a drone, Gabe, flying through free air space."

"It's either that or abandon it."

Another expulsion of air. "Okay, let me tee her up. I need you to manually configure some stuff on the Hunter's system."

He glanced back at the looming stadium. "Hurry up. I want to get out of here before company shows."

She talked him through the commands and he tapped the screen.

"Okay, that's it," Elle said. "Lia, you have control."

"Got it," Lia answered. "I'll do my best. It might be a bit battered, but fingers crossed I can get it back to base."

Gabe stepped back and the Hunter lurched forward, stopped, moved again.

"I'll get the hang of it," Lia said fiercely. "It'll be best if I follow your Hunter, Gabe."

"Got it."

Just then, the propane tank ran out, plunging him into darkness. *Fuck.*

He sprinted toward his Hunter, he got the driver's side door open, and heard small bird-like screeches in the sky above him.

He yanked the door closed...just as tiny bodies

hurled themselves at it.

"Fuck me." He started the Hunter's engine. "Let's get home." He gave his teammates a glance. They were all slumped over, breathing labored from pain. His gut cramped into a hard knot.

His squad, his brothers, his family.

All hurt. Because of him.

Chapter Thirteen

"Doc Emerson, I wouldn't mind getting injured more often if I got to see your pretty face all day."

Emerson adjusted the scanner and shot Shaw a bland look. He was propped up in the infirmary bed, just fresh off his nano-med treatment. He looked rather dashing lounging there, and his grin said he knew it.

"You're awfully perky for someone who almost died." She smiled at him. "And played the hero."

He grimaced. "Shh. Or she'll get started again."

"You're a goddamned idiot, is what you are." Claudia scowled from the adjacent bed. Her face was still a little pale, her scratches almost done healing. "Jumped on me like I was some fucking damsel in distress."

He snorted. "Frost, no one would ever mistake you for a damsel. I was just trying to save a teammate."

"Didn't see you tackle Marcus or Cruz."

"Fuck, you're ornery. I was standing right next to you." Shaw huffed and sat back in the pillows. "Forget it. Next time, I'll let you take a grenade to the face."

Claudia flopped back as well. "It was stupid and misguided...but thanks."

A far as thank yous went, it was pretty grudging. Emerson saw the look of blank shock on Shaw's face and swallowed her own grin.

But as she glanced over at Marcus and Cruz, both of whom had flat out refused to get in a bed, her smile disappeared. They hadn't been injured enough for nanos, but it had been close. They still looked pretty battered and Marcus had a neat row of med glue on his head. He'd have another scar for his collection. Elle hovered nearby and Santha stood with her hands on her hips, scowling.

Reed lay in a bed, sedated, a regen patch fitted over his eye, lights blinking on it. She was damned lucky they had an optical regen machine, otherwise Reed would have lost his eye. The damage had been too extensive even for the nano-meds. He'd need several treatments with the regen patch, but he'd keep his eye and see just as well as before.

Gabe had helped bring his injured team members in, then he'd disappeared. The entire time he hadn't once looked at Emerson, he'd refused medical treatment, and ignored her when she'd called out to him. From what she'd heard, he'd locked himself in his quarters and wasn't letting anyone in.

God, Hell Squad had been battered before, but not this badly. Maybe a part of her had always seen them as invulnerable. But being with Gabe the last few months...she'd seen that they were just men— and a woman—under the tough reputation. Yes, they were good at fighting, were born protectors, but they needed support and protection too.

She sighed.

"Don't worry, Doc. We'll bounce back."

She glanced back at Shaw. "I hope so. Otherwise there'll be some very unhappy ladies."

Claudia made a rude noise. "Way I see it, King of the Quickies must leave a few of them unhappy."

Shaw scowled, one hand twisting in his sheets. "So help me, Frost, I'm going to—"

"Uh-uh." Emerson patted his sheet-covered leg. "No violence in the infirmary. You're supposed to be resting." She shot Claudia a pointed look. "Both of you."

She left them grumbling. She was beyond worried about Gabe and now that Hell Squad were on the mend, she needed to check on him.

As she neared Marcus, his blue gaze zeroed in on her. "You going to see him?"

"Yes."

"He took risks tonight." Marcus' tone made it clear he wasn't happy.

Gabe may have taken risks, but he hadn't paid the price for it. Her chest tightened. His friends had. And she knew Gabe would have trouble dealing with that.

"Oh, and he quit," Marcus added.

She started. "What?"

"He quit the squad. Wouldn't say anything else."

She closed her eyes. "I'll talk to him."

"I never wanted him off the team. I just want Gabe—the steady, fucking excellent soldier—back."

"He's not the same man he was a few months back, Marcus. None of us are the same." And she suspected before the aliens were done, they'd all be forced to do things to survive, things they'd never have contemplated in their lives before the invasion.

Emerson headed down the tunnel. Gabe wasn't going to let her in. She was going to have to barge in and make him see reason.

She stopped at the comp lab. As always, she rolled her eyes at the sign on the door—*Shh, genius at work.* The inside was a chaotic mess. Desks topped with comps filled most of the space, and Noah's team of geeks worked at their computers. The rest of the place was overflowing with computer parts, tools, wiring and other electronic things she couldn't identify.

Noah looked up from his messy desk. Today his long, dark hair swung loose, brushing his shoulders. "Doc."

"Hey, Noah. I need a favor."

He set down...whatever it was he was working on, and inclined his head.

"Gabe's locked in his quarters, won't let anyone in. Can you code in my print so I can talk to him?"

"Heard Hell Squad got hit pretty hard. And Gabe brought them all home."

She nodded. "He shouldn't be alone right now."

"All right." Noah tapped his screen. "Done." He paused. "Sure you want to take on a brooding, angry solider like Gabe?"

She lifted her chin. "Yes."

Noah sat back. "Ah, it's like that, is it? Never picked Elle and Marcus. Santha and Cruz, yeah, they go together like microchips on a motherboard. You and Jackson...that I didn't see coming, either."

"I'm in love with him." God, saying the words aloud made her feel a bit dizzy.

Noah smiled. "He's a goddamned lucky man. Go get him."

Emerson hurried down to the section where Gabe's quarters were. She stood in front of his door, took a deep breath, and entered.

It was dark.

His quarters were just one large room—bunk against one wall, postage-stamp-size kitchenette in the back corner, one sofa making a lounge area opposite a comp screen.

He sat on the couch, still in his blood-splattered armor. He didn't turn his head.

"Go away, Emerson."

His voice was flat, dead, empty.

She decided to get mad. It wasn't hard. She was mad he was hurt, mad he wouldn't let her check him, mad he'd quit Hell Squad.

"Your team needs you and you're sitting here in the dark feeling sorry for yourself?"

He turned his head now, his jaw tight. "I said leave."

God, she really wanted to check him over. She could see the chest panel of his armor was badly damaged. He had to have injuries under there.

"You should be in the infirmary, if not for yourself, for your squad."

"They aren't my squad. Not anymore. And they sure as hell don't need me."

Her heart beat heavier. "You quit."

"Yeah. They're better off without me."

"You've been a key part of Hell Squad since Day One, Gabe..."

"I'm no good for them," he burst out.

She sucked in a breath. "That's not—"

"I almost got them all killed." His yelled words echoed in the small room. He clenched his hands and pressed them to his forehead. "Marcus has just found Elle. Cruz has a baby on the way. And they were both almost dead bodies because of me. Reed's eye—"

"Is okay." She didn't say anything else. She recognized that he needed to get this out.

"I didn't stay with the team, didn't work with them, didn't have their backs. I let a fucking raptor lure me into a trap like a green academy recruit."

"Gabe, please, listen to me. The mission went wrong, and it sounds like you made a bad choice, for the right reasons. But your team members, they'll recover, they're recovering right this instant. You're a vital part of that team."

"Not anymore."

His cold tone said he wouldn't be budged. God, she'd have better luck talking to a rock.

His gaze hit hers. "I'm better alone. Always have been. No more feelings. I'm not letting them drive me anymore."

She stilled. "What are you saying?"

"I've let all this fucking ugly angriness drive me

143

to be an idiot. Can't let that happen anymore. Those army doctors who enhanced me, made me stronger, they warned me that the best soldiers didn't feel. Don't let anyone too close. " His gaze was even and direct. "We're done, too, Emerson. It was never going to work, anyway. It's better you stay away from me." He turned away from her.

She knew he was hurting, but his words were still a blow. That he would throw away what they had with such ease. "Gabe—"

"Fuck. Just go, Emerson. I don't want you here. I don't want you pushing and pushing, expecting things from me I don't have to give to you."

She closed her eyes. The pain was excruciating, making her numb inside. Hadn't a part of her always worried that Gabe just didn't feel what she did? Apparently, she'd been right.

She didn't say anything else. She pressed a hand to her chest, like it would keep her bleeding heart in place and stumbled out of his room.

She didn't want to go to her quarters, or the infirmary. And she didn't want to see anyone else.

When she saw patients, she was always upbeat, wore a brave face. But right now, she couldn't pretend everything was going to be all right.

She started running, with no idea where she was headed.

***

Emerson sat near the raised vegetable beds in the hydroponic gardens, her arms wrapped around her upraised knees. Normally, she enjoyed visiting here. It always smelled fresh and green, and Old Man Hamish always ensured the plants were lush and thriving.

She wasn't letting herself think or feel. If she sat still and just enjoyed her surroundings, kept her mind blank, it almost worked.

Almost.

Footsteps. Someone sat down beside her and then someone else on the other side of her. She opened her eyes.

Elle and Santha.

Emerson heaved out a sigh.

"I take it that it didn't go well with Gabe?" Santha asked.

"No." Her voice was a jerky whisper.

"Want to talk about it?" Elle asked.

"He...doesn't want me."

Santha snorted. "Sure he does. He'd just afraid, Emerson. He has been since he lost Zeke."

"Or maybe before that. Since the army made him different," Elle added.

Emerson rubbed her cheek on her knee. "He doesn't want me pushing at him."

"Maybe, but he needs it." Santha shifted. "He's just too alpha to admit he's scared spitless. Gabe strikes me as the guy who thinks he has to be the perfect super-soldier all the time. Hell Squad relies on his enhanced senses in the field, his strength, his spooky ability to sneak up on the bad guys. He feels if he's anything less than perfect, he's failed them."

"He's been floundering since Zeke died," Elle said quietly. "He needs you, Emerson."

"It hurts," she whispered.

"Love does," Santha pronounced.

Emerson's mind, and her heart, shied away from the word. "Gabe's a grown man. He has to decide what he really wants. I can't be his quick fix to get by. Not anymore." She straightened. "I should get back to the infirmary. I have work to do."

Santha raised a brow. "It's always work with you, isn't it?"

Emerson stiffened. Where had she heard that before? "We don't all have hearts and rainbows like the two of you." She pushed to her feet.

The other women rose, too.

"If you're looking for hearts and rainbows from Gabe, then I'm not surprised you're here nursing a broken heart." Santha's words were cool and matter-of-fact.

"He's not that kind of guy," Elle added.

"No, he's not," Santha continued. "Doc, if you want easy, then you leave him alone from now on. Gabe will never be easy or comfortable. He'll always be intense and dangerous. If you keep expecting easy, you'll break him."

"Break him?" Emerson spluttered. "He dumped me!"

Santha waved a dismissive hand. "He's just running scared and being an idiot. Are you really going to give up on him so easily?"

That knocked the fight out of Emerson. She trembled. "I'm in love with him."

Relief flashed through Santha's pale-green eyes. Elle was beaming.

"Good. Then you need a plan of attack to bring him to his senses." Santha squeezed Emerson's shoulder. "Sometimes these alpha soldiers need saving from themselves."

Elle laughed. "Look who's talking." Elle ignored the face Santha pulled, and looked at Emerson. "Make him work a little."

Santha eyed Emerson's lab coat. "He ever see you in anything other than that lab coat?"

"He's seen me naked." God, how long had it been since she'd dressed up? Worn something to make herself feel good? "Besides, he really digs the lab coat."

"I have an idea," Elle said with a wide smile.

Santha cocked a hip. "And I happen to know that Mr. Broody is attempting to drink himself into a mindless stupor in the rec room."

Oh? So Gabe wasn't still brooding in his room.

Santha nodded. "When we're done with you, you'll bring him to his knees."

"And his senses," Elle added.

Emerson wasn't sure if she should be excited or afraid. But she knew she couldn't give up on Gabe.

Chapter Fourteen

Gabe knocked back another shot and slammed the glass down on the makeshift bar.

Beside him, Shaw did the same, then grimaced. "Okay, I think that's enough of this rotgut."

The homebrewed liquor wasn't smooth. It burned all the way down, but at least it was working to cloud Gabe's head. That was enough for him.

He nodded at the bartender. "Again."

Shaw heaved a sigh.

"You wanted to have a good time," Gabe said. "Maybe I'll get lucky, too."

Shaw made a choking noise and Gabe grimly drank his next shot. He had absolutely no interest in any of the soldier bunnies flitting around the rec room. He didn't give a shit if some of the women in the base were frank about the fact they enjoyed sex, and liked it even more with a soldier. In fact, he found the attitude refreshing.

But he had zero interest in any woman...except one.

Shaw coughed and spoke, his voice sounding strangled. "Holy hell. You need to check out the babe who just walked in."

Vaguely curious, Gabe glanced at the door. And almost swallowed his tongue.

Emerson had just strode in. She stood, hands on her hips, eying the room.

She was wearing her lab coat, but that's where anything usual ended. Her hair was a sleek cloud of blonde around her face, her eyes were rimmed with something dark that made them look even larger than normal, and her lips were wild red. Her skirt was black, and tight, and while it ended demurely at her knees, there was nothing fucking demure about it. It hugged every single one of her curves. Her top—and there wasn't much of it—was red and strapless, and cupped her breasts like a lover's hands. Her outfit ended with red heels that looked like lethal weapons.

Shaw let out a low whistle. "The doc looks miiiighty fine." The sniper slapped a hand to his chest. "Well, since you said you guys are over, I think I'll offer to buy her a drink."

"Shut it, Baird," Gabe growled. He noticed most of the male heads in the room had turned toward the doc. His pulse was hammering in his ears and he couldn't drag his gaze off her. Without thinking, he shot to his feet and strode over to her.

When she saw him, her face smoothed out and she cocked a hip.

"What do you think you're doing?" he said furiously.

"Enjoying myself."

"You're dressed like...like..."

Her eyes narrowed. "Like a woman looking for

someone who won't take me for granted? Someone who'll man up and commit?" She leaned closer. "Someone who isn't a coward?"

Gabe gritted his teeth. He'd told her they were over. That meant she could fuck whoever the hell she wanted.

Goddammit it, no.

She tossed her head back. "I plan to grab a drink. Maybe find someone to dance with."

"You want to dance? We'll dance." He gripped her arm and dragged her over to the unofficial dance floor.

The one couple swaying to the music of the two guys playing guitar saw them coming. One look at Gabe's face and the dancers took off. The musicians faltered for a second, until Gabe looked their way. The music resumed with gusto.

He pulled a stiff and pissed-looking Emerson into his arms. Gabe didn't dance. Ever. He swayed a bit to the beat, which was all he could manage.

"Why are you doing this, Gabe?"

He felt the muscles in his shoulders flex. Damn if he could find any words to explain himself.

"You were pretty clear you don't want to be with me. That you weren't willing to take the risk. But you don't want anyone else to have me, either?"

His hands tightened on her arms.

She sighed. A broken sound that cut through him deeper than a laser.

"I'm falling in love with you, Gabe. How's that for honesty?"

He stilled, his hands digging into her arms.

She looked up at him, her gaze traveling over his face. Then the expectant look on her face fell. "You'd look less scared if a pack of canids charged into the room." She started to pull away from him.

He didn't let her go. "I *am* scared."

She went rigid, then slowly relaxed. "You don't have to work it out alone, big guy." Her voice was quiet. She held out a hand. "I've never been in love, either. Let's work it out together."

He stared at her slim fingers. "I'm...not good at this. And I'm not like other men."

She smiled. "I know. That's why I love you."

Damn. His heart hit his ribs so hard it hurt. She loved him? Dr. Emerson Green loved a rough, risky grunt like him?

"I'm dangerous. I don't even know everything the army did to me. I don't want you hurt."

"That's the one thing I know you'd never do, Gabe. You fight for everyone else, but never for yourself. Sometimes you have to just have a little faith and trust, and take a leap."

She was right. It was time he trusted the people around him. He grabbed her hand and pulled it against his chest. Her eyes turned luminous.

He hauled her closer. "We do this, I won't let you go again. You'll be mine."

"Good," she murmured.

He decided it was time everyone knew Emerson Green was his.

He scooped her up in his arms. She laughed, sliding her arm across his shoulders. Around them, the room erupted in catcalls and whistles.

"Where are you taking me, big guy?"

He lowered his voice. "I want to fuck you while you wear only those shoes."

She sucked in a breath.

"And your lab coat."

***

Gabe did the calculations. His room was closer.

He slammed the door open and as soon as he kicked it shut, he had Emerson up against the wall, his lips devouring hers.

His hands shaped her hips, then slid up under her skirt. Her glorious curves were bare beneath. No underwear. *Hell.*

He found the fastening on her skirt. She was making those little breathy sounds that drove him crazy. It took him a few seconds to yank the skirt off her. Her poor excuse for a top followed. He groaned. "You are so beautiful, and so sexy you drive me out of my mind."

Her hands dug into his shoulders. "Gabe."

Lifting her up, he carried her to the bed and lowered her down. It took him a few seconds to strip off his clothes, then he was lowering himself onto her. He pulled one of her thighs up and around his hip.

She writhed against him. "Don't make me wait any—"

There was no more waiting. In one swift move, he thrust into her.

Her head flew back and she cried out his name.

He buried himself balls deep. He needed her warmth around him. She clung to him, her arms and legs wrapping around him. He felt those wicked heels digging into his ass.

As he moved inside her, she made those little cries again. "Oh, you fill me up."

And she filled him too—her light filled the hollow emptiness inside him. She helped him chase out the dark.

He rode her hard and fast, and she welcomed every powerful thrust, her hands roaming over every inch of him she could reach.

He felt her orgasm coming in the tightening of her body and his own growing in the electric shocks flicking up his spine. He leaned down and kissed her.

He thrust again and she came. He swallowed her wild cry.

A moment later, he followed her, groaning her name.

Chest heaving, he buried his face in the side of her neck. He'd only been without her for hours, but even that had ripped him up.

She was here, in his arms. Every gorgeous, sexy inch of her. She was so far inside him, he'd never get her out, didn't want to get her out.

Emerson was all his.

***

Emerson's internal alarm told her it was morning. She'd learned to trust it, as there was no sunlight in the base to give her body the cues.

She snuggled deeper into Gabe's chest. Their legs were tangled together and every inch of her felt lazy. His big hand was tracing her back and she smiled at the way he touched her. With a hint of reverence.

Something started beeping, cutting into her sense of peace. Communicator. *Dammit.* "Is that mine, or yours?"

He moved, reaching out an arm. "Mine."

She turned, pressing her lips to his skin. Hmm, all that bare chest. He was talking into the communicator, his voice rumbling through his chest. Then his tone hardened and Emerson frowned and sat up, pushing her hair out of her face.

"We'll be there." He snapped the communicator shut.

"What is it?" she asked.

"Santha's top guy, Devlin, found something."

"The Genesis Facility?"

"Marcus didn't say. Maybe. We need to get to Ops." Gabe pressed a kiss to her mouth, lingered with a groan, then climbed out of bed. He pulled on his clothes. "Sounds like this Devlin got a bit beat up getting out of raptor territory."

Emerson leaped up. "Why didn't anyone call me?" She looked for her clothes.

"Don't know."

She eyed her skirt and strapless top and grimaced. "I need to stop by my quarters."

He followed her gaze. "Hell, yeah. No way are

you wearing that outfit into Ops."

"Not even the shoes?" she teased.

"No," he growled. "You'll have to make do knowing I still have marks from those heels on my ass."

Ten minutes later—and now sensibly clothed— Emerson followed Gabe into the Operations Area. She had her field kit over her shoulder. They found Santha, Hell Squad and General Holmes in a conference room, gathered around a glossy table. Elle and Santha both winked at Emerson, wide smiles flashing on their faces.

Then Emerson focused on the stranger in the room.

This had to be the mysterious Devlin. He was tall and lean, with dark hair that had a hint of curl. As he glanced her way, she saw his eyes were so dark they looked black. He had a hell of a face. Not because it was perfect, but because it made her think of late-night sins and fallen angels.

He was also bleeding from the head. It had stained his neck and soaked his gray shirt.

She hurried over to him. "Hi. I'm your friendly doctor, here to scan, poke and prod you." She opened her backpack.

He didn't smile, but something resembling amusement flared in his dark eyes. "Anything I can do to talk you out of the poking and prodding part?" He had a crisp British accent.

"Nope." She lifted her m-scanner. "I took an oath and all of that. Besides, I get a kick out of poking and prodding." She set the scanner to work on his head. "So, you're Devlin?"

"Yes." His gaze went over her shoulder. "Devlin Gray."

"Dev's become the backbone of my intel team," Santha said. "He's so good at sneaking around he makes the rest of us look like toddlers taking baby steps."

"Well, Devlin. You haven't been in for any medical checks since you arrived. I'll expect you in the next few days."

He raised a brow. "Yes, Doctor."

Emerson didn't buy his meek tone for a second. "You found the Genesis Facility?" She held her breath.

"I think I've found it. I rigged a hand scanner to find this alien liquid. I found a lot of traces of it heading north out of the city. Lot of raptor patrols heading north, too."

"Looks like the tanks in North Sydney were just a holding area," Santha said.

Emerson's scanner beeped. She studied the results. Nothing major. He didn't even need nano-meds. She showed him a tube of med-gel, then squeezed it onto his wound.

"Today, I took a Darkswift north," Devlin continued.

"Stole a Darkswift," Marcus interrupted darkly.

Devlin shrugged. "Borrowed." He appeared unconcerned at the bark of Hell Squad's sergeant. "An hour or so north of here, I found something. Up in the Hunter Valley."

"Wine region, right?" Shaw said. "Vineyards everywhere."

Devlin nodded. "Yeah. It was a former coal mining area way back. But once the mines were played out, the mining companies rehabilitated the area. Their methods got so good, you can hardly tell the area's been touched. There were also a couple of coal-fired powers stations and they fell into disuse and disrepair. At one of the stations, I found this." He nodded at Santha, who tapped the comp screen.

An image filled the large screen on the wall.

Gasps filled the room.

Emerson looked up, her hands freezing over the cut on Devlin's head. "What the hell is that?"

Chapter Fifteen

Emerson stared at the giant orange dome that was easily visible from the air. It was huge, and slightly translucent. Enough to see there was something inside of it.

"The readings for the alien fluid are off the charts," Devlin said.

"The Genesis Facility." It had to be. "It's enormous." Emerson felt dismay fill her. So many people had to be trapped in there.

"It is, but—" Devlin's dark gaze moved around the room "—it isn't well guarded. Two raptor patrols, that's it."

"They think we're too far away." Gabe was scowling.

Marcus stepped forward. "But we're not." He glanced at the general. "When do we go in?"

General Holmes stared at the orange dome, his jaw tight. "As soon as possible. Take Squad Nine and Three with you."

"Three?" Marcus grimaced. "Devlin said the dome isn't well guarded, so we shouldn't need—"

"Take them." Holmes' tone said he wasn't going to argue. "If we're lucky, we'll have some survivors to bring home, so the extra hands will help."

Marcus gave a short nod. "Fine."

Emerson hid her smile. Squad Three was...unique. While Hell Squad were heroes and deadly fighters, Squad Three were known as the Berserkers. They were all a little...crazy. Dangerous and crazy.

The next few hours were a whirl. Emerson barely saw Gabe. She was too busy getting her small team of med technicians ready to head into the field. She'd selected Phillip and his boyfriend, Rick. They were steady and worked well together. The final member was a female paramedic who'd been in the field once or twice. It was clear Molly was nervous but also determined. They were all finishing fastening their armor.

"Double check your supplies." Emerson worked through her field backpack. "We'll need to treat any survivors." If there *were* survivors. She hadn't forgotten that the three people they'd removed from the tanks at the Luna Park lab had died. "And drugs to euthanize those we can't help."

It was a grim reality. The doctor in her wanted to save everyone, but they just didn't have the resources or understanding to care for those too far along in the raptor transformation.

"Ready?" she asked.

The three of them straightened, and nodded.

The landing pads were alive with frantic activity. Four Hawks were waiting, their rotors spinning.

Hell Squad stood near one, checking their gear. Elle and Santha were there saying good bye to their men. Roth Masters, the leader of Squad Nine, stood talking with his mostly female squad by the second Hawk. He was another big soldier with muscular, broad shoulders, a rugged face, and sandy hair cut short. The third Hawk would remain empty. The pilot would stay back from the dome on standby, ready to be called in if there were more survivors than they'd estimated.

In front of the final Hawk stood Squad Three—the Berserkers.

All men, all really large men. Most of them had beards or at least some heavy scruff on their faces. Three of them were brothers with Maori heritage, evident in their strong faces, dark skin and tough bodies. The leader of the squad, Tane Rahia, stood a little taller and leaner than his brothers, his long dark hair in dreadlocks that he pulled back and tied at the base of his neck. Most of them didn't wear armor on their arms, so lots of biceps bulged, covered in black ink.

She'd heard not all of them had military backgrounds, but that they were vicious fighters and famed for their wild, berserker fighting on the battlefield. And they couldn't always be trusted to follow orders. She'd patched them up...a lot...and knew they were just as tough as Hell Squad.

Emerson led her team over to Hell Squad. Marcus and the others called out hellos. Gabe yanked her to his side.

"Before we take off, I have something for you." He held out his hand.

Emerson saw a silver chain resting on his palm.

A polished stone pendant in a brilliant blue dangled from it.

"It's the same color as your eyes," he said.

God, how could she have ever believed the man wasn't able to express himself? She took the necklace and fingered the pretty stone. "It's beautiful. Help me put it on?"

He secured it around her neck and Emerson was sorry when she had to tuck it under her armor.

"I've never asked you, why polished stones?"

He shrugged. "They make me think of you."

"Oh?"

"They're pretty and people in the past used to believe different stones had healing properties. You're a healer."

She pressed her palms to his chest. "I love you."

He dropped his forehead to hers. "Doc, I'm still not sure being with me is the best thing for you, but I think I'd like you to show me what this love thing is all about."

She smiled. "You got it, big guy."

A clearing throat interrupted them.

Marcus was aboard the Hawk and was leaning out the door. The others had boarded. "We have some alien butt to kick."

She nodded and glanced up at Gabe. "Talk after?"

"After." His voice lowered. "And we'll do more than talk. Stay safe." He lifted her up and boosted her into the quadcopter.

The flight north was tense. The Hawk had an electrified air, everyone edgy and twitchy.

Emerson's team watched Hell Squad prepare. Triple-checking weapons, going over battle plans. Reed was sorting through an obscenely large supply of explosives. Out the side window, Emerson could just make out the shimmers of the other Hawks. With their illusion systems up, they were just blurs in the sky.

"We have a visual." Finn called out from the cockpit. "Damn. Never seen anything like it."

They all moved, shifting or arching necks to see out of the windows.

Holy cow. It was even bigger than she'd imagined from the image. The dome looked like a perfect hemisphere of amber. It was darker at the base, where black vein-like growths were visible in it. At the top, it was a clearer orange. It was almost as high as the old cooling towers of the abandoned power station beside it.

Marcus, one arm above his head gripping a handhold on the roof, swiveled to face them. "We'll be landing in a few minutes."

Emerson already felt the quadcopter starting its descent.

"Hell Squad? Ready to go to hell?" Marcus asked.

"Hell, yeah." The squad yelled. Emerson raised her voice to join them. "The devil needs an ass-kicking!"

The Hawks touched down.

Emerson turned to Molly, Rick and Phillip. "Stay close to Hell Squad. Don't get separated." She tapped her ear. "You need anything, ask Elle."

They nodded, all of them securing their medical packs on their backs.

Gabe helped Emerson down. He touched her cheek for a fleeting second, a huge flash of emotion swimming in his gray eyes, then he turned and lifted his carbine.

They'd landed a short distance away from the dome, but it still dominated the landscape, rising up like a giant orange sun.

The grass in the field was long and wading through it was hard work. Ahead of her, Hell Squad didn't seem fazed. To the right, Roth and his team were moving ahead. To the left, the Berserkers charged forward, intent on reaching the dome.

As they neared the structure, Emerson heard deep-throated yells from the Berserkers. She slowed and glanced back. The grass near them was waving madly, and an animal's scream filled the air. It raised the hairs on her arms. *What the hell?* Squad Three started firing their carbines.

Suddenly, a large creature leaped out of the grass and crashed into one of the Berserkers. Emerson saw a flash of feathers, and wicked clawed feet. The animal looked like the velociraptors she'd seen in the history databases.

The fallen man's teammates rushed to help him. Emerson's heart was beating so fast she felt like it might burst from her chest.

"Velox," Gabe murmured. "Fast, smart bastards."

"Keep moving," Marcus called out.

"He might need medical help," Emerson said.

Marcus's smile was a tiny lift of his lips. "Don't think so."

She turned back. The Berserker had taken down the velox. The man was standing, blood all over him, laughing like a lunatic.

"Right," Emerson said with a shake of her head.

Ahead, she heard more carbine fire. Squad Nine had engaged a raptor patrol.

Gabe moved in closer to Emerson. They rushed ahead, and she could tell Hell Squad were itching to help Nine.

Which, apparently, the other squad didn't need it. Moments, later, Roth and his team had finished wiping out the patrol. Large raptor bodies littered the ground.

A deep voice with a New Zealand accent came through the earpiece. "Steele, we've spotted the other raptor patrol. Heading to engage."

"Roger that, Tane," Marcus answered. "Good hunting." He faced Hell Squad with a frown. "All right, there's a chance the aliens will send back up. Let's head inside and get this done."

As a group, they moved toward the strange, large doorway into the dome. Marcus nodded to Reed.

The tall man moved forward and fixed a tiny metal object to the door. He pressed a button on it and stepped back.

Nothing happened.

Emerson eyed the others, but they were still watching the door. She looked back...and saw the metal object was moving. A bright-orange glow appeared below it.

A laser cutter.

It moved in a large arch. When it clicked off, Reed stepped forward again and snatched it up. Then he pressed one boot to the dome and kicked.

The door fell inward.

Emerson sucked in a deep breath and followed Hell Squad inside.

***

Gabe stepped inside the dome. Damn, he didn't like this place.

There were hundreds, maybe thousands, of tanks lined up in rows. The filtered light shining through the dome cast a strange orange glow over everything, and the atmosphere felt wrong. It was more humid inside than outside, and it left his chest a little tight.

Emerson had her scanner out. "The oxygen level in the air is a little low, but still in tolerable range." She frowned. "It must help promote the transformation."

"All right, Doc, this is your show," Marcus said. "Tell us what you need us to do."

She nodded, pulling small rolls from her backpack. "Everyone take a roll of stickers. Take a row of tanks and mark a tank red if the occupant shows obvious raptor traits. Anyone who still looks completely human gets a green sticker. Orange for any you're not sure about. My team and I will come along and scan them all to double-check and set any oranges to green or red."

"Then what?" Claudia asked.

"Green, we'll pull out and see if we can save them."

"And red?" Reed asked.

"We've brought drugs to euthanize them. There are ports in the tanks, so we'll inject the drug directly into the tank fluid."

Gabe admired her steady, non-nonsense tone. But he knew her well enough now to hear the pain under her words. He knew that being unable to save them all cut her deep.

They all got to work. Roth and his team joined them to help. Tane and his squad were outside on patrol.

Soon, all the tanks were marked with colored stickers. Hell Squad began the grim task of hauling bodies out of the green tanks.

Gabe waited as Reed passed him body, after body. Most of them never moved.

Those who dragged in rasping breaths, he carried over to Emerson or one of her paramedics for them to tend to. Soon, there was a small, drenched, and shivering group of survivors. They huddled together, confused and upset. One of Emerson's paramedics spoke to them in a soothing voice, reassuring them as he checked their vital signs.

Emerson took on the task of administering the drugs to those patients in the tanks who they couldn't help.

It was clear to Gabe that those people were suffering. Inside the tanks, he saw faces caught in grimaces of pain, and others jerking spasmodically.

But it didn't make Emerson's task any easier. He saw the way her shoulders slumped and the way she braced herself before she injected each tank.

He watched her approach another tank. The occupant inside clearly sensed her and attacked the glass, kicking and hitting. The female face behind the orange-tinted glass was a mask of rage and pain.

Emerson flinched, but her hands were rock steady as she injected the drug.

Soon the tank's occupant stopped fighting. The woman's movements slowed until she hung in the fluid, still and silent.

Emerson pulled in a breath and moved to the next tank.

Tonight, Gabe would be Emerson's safe haven from the darkness. He'd hold her, make love to her, and make sure she was too tired to have nightmares.

Suddenly, gunfire echoed through the dome. Gabe spun. Raptor gunfire. A second later, he heard carbines returning fire.

"Hell Squad, western side of the dome," Elle's voice came through the comm. "Raptors must have been lying in wait and hiding their signatures. There are fifteen of them."

Fuck, an ambush. He glanced at Emerson. She was shouting at her med techs who were moving to surround the survivors. She had her laser pistol clutched in her hand. With a final look at her, Gabe stormed through the tanks, catching up with Marcus and Reed.

Then Hell Squad did what they did best.

Working together, they weeded out the raptors. Gabe, Reed and Marcus switched to combat knives, fighting up close. Shaw stayed back, picking off raptors who dared pop their heads out from their hiding places. Claudia and Cruz were flanking the raptors, pushing them toward the rest of Hell Squad.

They'd just taken down the last raptor, all of them breathing heavily, when Emerson's scream cut across the comm.

Gabe froze in the act of wiping his knife clean. When she screamed again and he heard the grunts of the raptor language, he spun and ran in her direction.

"Gabe!"

Marcus was right behind him and he heard the rest of Hell Squad running too.

Gabe had enough presence of mind to skid to a halt before he reached her and lift his weapon. He rounded the last row of tanks.

Ahead, the one-eyed raptor was holding Emerson in front of him, dragging her backward.

The bastard. Fear was a rock in Gabe's chest.

She was fighting, kicking, and twisting her body. But her struggles were nothing to the large raptor. He dragged her around another tank and out of view.

Gabe took a step forward, then paused.

"Gabe." Marcus was right there beside him. Cruz flanked him on the other side.

"That fucker has Emerson." Gabe's voice was a harsh rasp. "I have to get her back."

"*We* will," Marcus said. "By working together."

Gabe closed his eyes, trying to calm the rampant, out-of-control feeling inside him. Emerson had helped him learn that working together made him stronger, not weaker.

He looked at his team and nodded. "Together."

Claudia squeezed his arm. Shaw slapped his shoulder. Reed nodded.

Gabe looked forward, his hand's tightening on his weapon. "Let's get her back."

Chapter Sixteen

Terror clawed at Emerson.

Memories assaulted her, but this time was different. This time, she was fighting back. She kicked and twisted her body, making it as hard for the raptor as she could.

He made a guttural sound and dropped her on her knees. Before she could move, he swung a large palm and backhanded her.

Pain exploded in her cheek and she cried out, her eyes watering. In that second, she was back at that other time this alien had kept her captive. The time he'd beaten the fight out of her.

That wasn't going to happen now. Not this time.

Surrounded by the tanks, and the shadows floating inside them, her anger burned like a flame. And somewhere nearby was Gabe, her man, who would be going crazy knowing this one-eyed bastard had her.

The raptor grabbed the back of her armor and dragged her forward. When he finally stopped, he tossed her roughly on the ground and she caught herself on her hands and knees before she smacked the concrete.

"You are...intelligent."

Her head jerked up. Hearing him speak English in his raspy voice gave her shivers.

"I have seen...you are a healer."

"Yes. And I'll use everything I have to end this." She stabbed a finger at the closest tanks.

He smiled. At least, she thought the baring of sharp teeth was supposed to be a smile.

"Can't end this."

Arrogant bastard. She bit her tongue. Mouthing off at him wouldn't help. She needed to use those brains he'd admired to get herself out of here.

"You will make a good addition to the Gizzida," he said.

What? Panic surged, closing her throat.

He barked out a command and one of the raptors by his side reached up and opened the top of an empty tank. Then One Eye started dragging her toward it.

"You intrigue me." He nodded to another raptor who stepped forward, holding what she guessed was a raptor version of a syringe. The center of the bone-like needle was filled with orange liquid. "A healer, like me."

Emerson struggled. "No way. I like being human."

"You will—" he frowned, clearly searching for a word "—forget." He ran his hand over her blonde hair. "It will be a shame to lose this."

She kicked out at his knees. Hard. This time she was fighting for herself. For Gabe and their love. For her humanity.

She kicked again. The raptor stumbled and let

out a grunt. He grabbed at her and she dodged, slapping his arm away.

Then he grabbed her by her hair and yanked her up.

Tears pricked her eyes, her scalp burning. He held her up until their gazes met.

"You will be stronger. More intelligent. With your skills, you can help us."

"Never." But even Emerson heard the desperate tremble in her voice.

"Once, I was like you. Weak. Afraid. Now...I am Gizzida."

Gabe's face flashed in her mind. She'd just claimed him. She wanted more.

Screw this. She twisted and slammed her palm up into the raptor's face.

She surprised him, and her palm landed hard on what passed for his nose. Something broke inside, and blood gushed. He dropped her, his roar reverberating through the tanks.

Emerson landed hard, pain shooting up her tailbone. But she scrambled up, knocked into the nearby raptor, and snatched the needle out of his claws. Then she swung around and slammed the needle into her tormentor's good eye.

He howled. He swung out with a closed fist, catching her temple. The blow sent her skidding across the floor.

It took a second for Emerson to draw a breath. When she looked up, One Eye towered over her. He yanked the syringe out. His eye was streaming blood, but it was fixated on her, so she guessed he could still see. He growled and snatched an alien weapon off the nearest raptor soldier.

Then he headed her way, lifting the gun.

Her stomach clenched. *Oh, God.* Her hand went to her neck and closed over the necklace Gabe had given her. *I'm so sorry, Gabe.*

Gunfire sounded. She flinched. But there was no pain.

She looked up.

And saw Gabe, surrounded by Hell Squad, bearing down on them.

The raptors were returning fire, but were being picked off one by one by the human soldiers.

The tank behind her shattered, and a torrent of fluid washed over her. When she opened her eyes, she saw Gabe launch himself at One Eye. The raptor and the man fell to the floor, rolling.

Emerson scrambled over to them, staying low to dodge the gunfire. Gabe was on top of the raptor, pummeling the alien with steady, hard hits.

But from her vantage point, she saw One Eye draw a large, jagged knife and hold it by his side.

Emerson got her feet under her and dived.

The raptor raised his arm to strike Gabe, but Emerson grabbed his elbow, twisting the knife away from Gabe.

She struggled to hold the raptor's arm. God, he was strong. He shoved at her, staring at her with his bleeding eye. *Too strong.* Her muscles strained. The raptor turned the knife until it was pointed toward her chest. She felt her arms tremble under the pressure.

Then Gabe's arms surrounded her, his big hands covering hers.

Together, they pushed. They forced the blade back around and the raptor's eye widened, a hoarse sound escaping his throat.

Emerson and Gabe forced the blade into the raptor's chest. It sank deep. She watched his body twitch, then go still. His red eye closed.

Dead. It was over.

She spun and flung herself at Gabe. She wrapped around him, feeling his hard, solid presence. "Oh, God."

"Emerson." He buried his face in her hair.

His arms were so tight around her, she could barely breathe. She didn't care.

His hand tangled in her hair. "Jesus, when I saw he had you..."

"I'm okay." She cupped Gabe's tough, beloved face and kissed him.

He kissed her back, and she felt emotion pouring off him.

They were surrounded by hell, but right here, in each other's arms, they were making their own piece of heaven.

***

Gabe walked behind Emerson, staying within arm's reach, as they walked through the dome, checking the last of the tanks.

He wasn't letting her out of his sight. Not for a long time. Maybe not ever.

"Okay, two more tanks we need to empty." She pointed. "That one and that one."

Not far away, two of her team were overseeing the traumatized survivors. Some were sobbing, others just stared, shell-shocked. One man was rocking back and forth.

Up on the tank, Shaw heaved a teenaged boy out and handed him down. Gabe laid the boy on the ground and Emerson checked him. She sank back on her heels and shook her head.

"Last one," Roth called out from the next tank where one of his team was pulling out a woman.

Roth took the limp woman. The fluid was dripping off her. Suddenly, she snapped awake. She took one look around and hit out. She caught Roth in the face and he dropped her. She landed in a crouch, and in the next breath, launched herself at Roth.

Gabe raised a brow. Damn, for someone who'd been floating in a tank for who knew how long, she could move. Gabe watched as Roth countered the woman's well-trained moves. He was blocking her hits, trying not to hurt her, and he took a few head-turning blows.

She spun in a roundhouse kick and Roth caught her leg and twisted. He took her to the ground, holding her down with his bigger body. She bucked beneath him.

"Enough," Roth said sharply. "We're here to help you."

She slowed, but kept fighting.

"Dammit. I don't want to hurt you," Roth bit out.

"Tone it down or I'll have the doc knock you out."

"Date." The woman's voice was raspy, clearly not used for a long time.

"Date?" Roth frowned.

"What's the date?"

He rattled it off and the woman blanched. "No." She fell back on the ground, her gaze focused up at the dome. "No." A tortured whisper. "They invaded."

The fight went out of the woman and Roth's body softened as he pulled her up, murmuring quietly.

"What the hell is she talking about?" Gabe ground out.

Roth glanced up. "Not sure we want to know." When the woman started shivering, he hitched her. "For now, it'll have to wait."

"These poor people," Emerson murmured.

Gabe looked at her. She was watching the woman, then Emerson's gaze drifted to the tanks surrounding them, now filled with floating bodies no longer suffering and in pain.

"We did what we could," he said.

She gave a tired nod. "I need one of these tanks."

Gabe waved Marcus over and relayed her request. Marcus nodded. "I'll take care of it."

Emerson and Gabe headed toward the survivors. "They'll never be the same."

"No one's the same. They can make a new life for themselves if they choose." He squeezed her hand. He'd chosen. "Alien apocalypse or not, life can still be pretty fucking amazing."

She smiled. "Charmer."

He nodded at Shaw and Claudia who were now arguing over the best way to move one of the tanks. They were going head to head, arms waving in the air. "None of us are alone. Not unless we choose to be." He'd been on the loner path, but not anymore.

Emerson leaned her head against his arm for a second. "I need to supervise getting the survivors loaded into the Hawks."

"And I promised to help Reed set the explosives to blow this place sky high."

"See you soon?"

"Count on it."

Chapter Seventeen

Reed

Reed set the backfire charge at the base of a tank in the center of the dome. The aliens and their fucking facility could go to hell.

He moved along, judged the distance, and set another small charge. The round metal disc had two tiny windows on it. One showed a line of glowing blue and the other a line of glowing red. When the two lines met...boom.

The sobs of one of the survivors rang in his ears, making his jaw tight. So much damage, so much pain, so much heartache. He thought of another alien torture survivor. One who'd wept in his arms, big brown eyes drowning in pain. Yeah, he liked blowing things up, but this job he was doing now was mostly for her.

"Reed?" Gabe's deep voice on the comm. "Mine are all set."

"Cheers, bud. I have a couple more and then I'm finished."

"Tell me if you need any more help."

Reed smiled. Gabe already sounded more

mellow. All thanks to the love of a good woman. Reed thought a hard man like Gabe more than deserved all the softness and happiness the doc would give him.

Ahead, Reed saw the rest of his team wrestling one of the tanks out the door. There was a whole lot of cursing going with it. Damn, he was glad he'd found Hell Squad.

He'd spent months after the invasion traveling south from the Great Barrier Reef. Thanks to the aliens, his dream diving vacation had turned to hell. He'd heard rumors from other survivors about Blue Mountain Base, where any remaining military had gathered and were fighting back.

He missed his SEAL team. He hoped some of the boys and girls had made it. But other than his fellow SEALs, he'd not had many attachments. His elderly parents had passed a few years back, and while he'd never lacked for the company of women, there had never been a special one.

The water had been his mistress. And the outdoors. Anywhere he could breathe in fresh air. Freedom was a fundamental right he believed in to the bone. His hand tightened on the charge. He knew what it was like when someone stole it from you.

He pulled in a breath. He had a place at Blue Mountain Base and on Hell Squad, fighting these aliens out to steal humanity's freedom...and that felt pretty darn good.

And, if he was patient enough, he might also convince the woman who fascinated him to be his.

Reed shook his head and cursed mentally. She was a long way from ready for the force of what he had to offer. His fingers curled into fists. He had to have some control, and give her time.

He set the final charge.

Reed headed back to the group.

Marcus raised a brow. "All done?"

Reed nodded. "Say the word and this place will be smoldering ashes."

"Good."

"Shaw and Claudia need help with that tank?"

Marcus snorted. "You want to steer well clear of those two. I left them fucking arguing about how to get the damn thing into the Hawk." He jerked his head. "Help the doc get the last of the survivors loaded."

Reed helped carry an unconscious pre-teen boy out to the Hawks. Soon everyone was loaded and the Hawks lifted off. Reed lifted the controller in his hand and thumbed the button.

He made eye contact with Marcus. His boss nodded.

Ka-boom time. Reed pressed the button.

A second later, the Genesis Facility exploded. A huge blue ball rose into the air above the shattered dome. The heart of the cloud turned a brilliant red.

The secondary explosion ignited and the dome simply ceased to be. As the edge of the shockwave hit the copter, the Hawk rocked a little. Reed gripped the handle above his head.

For you, my brown-eyed girl.

***

"Last one settled." Emerson puffed out a breath and dropped into her office chair. Her very bones were aching with exhaustion.

She'd personally checked out the twenty-seven people they'd managed to extract from the tanks. They were all now tucked up in infirmary beds. Most were not sleeping soundly, except the ones she'd had to sedate. She suspected most of them wouldn't sleep soundly for a long, long time.

Emerson logged out of her comp. "I'm out of here."

Norah raised her brows. "Excuse me? Dr. Workaholic Green isn't going to spend the night hovering over her newest arrivals? Or poring over medical files? Working herself to the bone?"

Emerson shot her friend a mock-scowl. "Funny. And no. They have a good team watching over them, headed by an opinionated, sometimes-pain-in-the-ass nurse. And I have a man to get home to."

"And a fine hunk of man he is." Norah's eyes got a faraway look. "The man's intensity is a little on the scary side, but the way he looks at you...*damn*."

Yes. Emerson smiled to herself. Damn.

She raced back to her quarters and took a quick shower to wash the last of the mission away. She'd just finished tying her favorite silver robe around her when she heard someone moving about in her living area. She headed out and stopped in the doorway.

Gabe had showered, too. His black T-shirt clung

to his fabulous body and his jeans shaped his magnificent ass.

Mine. All mine.

He looked over his shoulder, his gaze drifting over her, the faintest smile on his lips. "Hi."

"Hi." She walked toward him. "How was the debrief?"

"Long. The patients?"

Her happiness dimmed. "We lost one. Some I had to sedate. They have a long way to go."

"But first they have to choose to fight for life."

"Yes." She smoothed her hands up his chest. For all the horrors of their new world, she was so incredibly happy life had given her Gabe Jackson. "I like you being here, big guy."

He gave her a slow smile that made her insides melt.

"I was thinking I'd make some space in my closet for your things." When he didn't say anything, nerves crept in. "That's if you *want* to move in, I just thought—"

He cupped her cheeks and nodded toward the door.

She saw the duffel bag she hadn't noticed before with a box beside it filled with a few things. Her tight chest eased. "Oh. Well, then."

"Already handed in my quarters, so you're stuck with me now," he said.

Emerson thought being stuck with Gabe Jackson was a pretty good situation to be in. When she saw a bandage peeking out above the neckline of his shirt, she frowned. "Are you hurt? Why didn't you tell me?" She yanked the neckline down.

"Not hurt." He covered her hands with his, and gently moved them aside. Then he ripped the bandage off and pulled the neckline down for her to see.

Her heart leaped into her throat. "Oh, Gabe."

Under the names of his grandmother and brother was a new word, etched into his skin in the same coiling script as the others. *Emerson.*

She traced the edge of it. "Who did this?"

"Shaw. Guy's pretty good."

"It's beautiful. Thank you." Gabe was *so* in love with her.

He caught his hands in her hair and dragged her head back. "Every time I look at you, there is so much I want to say."

"Just say it, Gabe. I don't expect you to turn into a talker. I just want you to be yourself."

He took a deep breath. "I love you, Emerson."

Warmth flooded her chest. "I know."

A line appeared on his brow. "How do you know?"

"Let's just say I'm getting pretty good at reading macho alpha male." She nipped his lips. "But it's still nice to hear you say it."

"I've never said that to any woman before."

Her breath hitched. "I love you too, big guy."

She kissed him. It started soft and turned hot in an instant. He dragged her closer, groaning into her mouth. Her fingers dug into his skin. She wondered if it would always be like this, one touch and she went up in flames.

Her front door slammed open.

"Dinner's served." Claudia strode in, carrying a tower of pizza boxes. "Don't ask me what I had to bribe the chef with to get these babies."

"I've got drinks." Shaw was holding a crate of homebrew beers. He scowled at Claudia's back. "I want to know what you bribed him with."

Marcus came next, his arm around a smiling Elle. "We brought dessert," the brunette said. "Cheesecake."

Cruz and Santha followed. "Didn't bring any food, but I brought this." Cruz held up his guitar.

Reed ambled in last. "My contribution." He held up a comp chip. "It's an old classic about a commando team who get taken out by an invisible alien in the jungle."

Emerson looked up and watched a scowling Gabe stare at his team. They were busy making themselves at home, slouching on chairs, popping the tops on the beers.

She nudged Gabe. "They love you, too."

He blinked, a riot of emotions in his eyes. "Yeah."

Emerson laughed and realized she felt the lightest she'd felt in a long time.

This was life right here. And family.

She snuggled into Gabe's warm strength. And love.

I hope you enjoyed Emerson and Gabe's story!

Hell Squad continues with REED, the story of Hell Squad's sexy Navy SEAL, Reed, and alien lab survivor, Natalya. Read on for a preview of the first chapter.

Don't miss out! For updates about new releases, action romance info, free books, and other fun stuff, sign up for my VIP mailing list and get your free copy of the Phoenix Adventures novella, *On a Cyborg Planet*.

Visit here to get started:

www.annahackettbooks.com

FREE DOWNLOAD

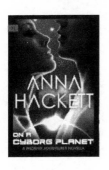

JOIN THE ACTION-PACKED ADVENTURE!

Formats: Kindle, ePub, PDF

Read the first chapter of Reed

"Moving in on the target now."

Reed MacKinnon kept his voice low as he murmured into his comms device. He crept forward silently on his belly, toward the edge of the roof of the ruined house.

Below, he heard a woman sobbing, a man shouting, and aliens snarling.

Carefully peering down, he saw the group of seven raptors towering over a human couple. The man and woman looked like they'd been on the move for a while. Their clothes were tattered and dirty, and they had a hungry, desperate look. And now they had aliens waving ugly scaled weapons in their faces.

Reed lined up his mayhem carbine. The weapon had a mini-missile launcher attached, but he wouldn't need that right now. Through his scope, he stared at one of the dinosaur-like humanoid's faces with its gray scales and red eyes. Nope, a good ol' laser shot to the head would be enough.

He waited patiently for his squad's leader to make the call. Reed couldn't see his teammates, but he knew they were nearby somewhere. Shaw would be looking down the laser scope of his long-range sniper rifle. Claudia would be silently bouncing on her heels, ready to rush in. Gabe would be a ghost, hiding in the shadows with his big-ass combat knife in hand. Cruz would be steady and calm, waiting for Marcus' command. And Marcus, he'd be gritting his teeth and pissed off, waiting for the right moment to hit these aliens and rescue the couple.

"Just leave us alone," the man below yelled.

One seven-foot-tall raptor kicked out with a huge, booted foot. He caught the man in the chest, sending him sprawling in the dirt.

"Don't!" The woman scrambled toward her partner, tangled blonde hair falling around her face. "You've taken everything. Our homes, our children, our planet. What more can you want from us?"

It was true. The raptors had come in their huge alien ships and annihilated life on Earth. They'd ruined the cities, decimated most of the population, stolen resources. But there was more they could take. The real, hideous reason they were here. Reed's gut roiled. Freedom was every man's right, and these bastards had flown halfway around the galaxy to take humanity's freedom away from them.

Reed stared down his scope. Well, theses human weren't about to roll over and make it easy. The aliens were going to get a hell of a fight.

One raptor soldier snagged the woman by the collar of her shirt and dragged her toward the black, squat-looking vehicle covered in spiked armor plating nearby.

"Shaw, on my command, take out the patrol leader, then the alien next to him." Marcus Steele's gravelly voice rasped over the comm. "Reed, you take out the big bastard on the right. Gabe and Claudia, move in and take out the other three. Cruz, you can have the guy holding the woman. I'll disable their vehicle and driver."

Battle calm flowed over Reed. Another few tense seconds passed. The woman was screaming at the top of her lungs now and her struggling husband got a kick to the head for his attempts to help his wife.

"Go," Marcus said.

Hell Squad burst into action.

A single laser blast and the head raptor fell to the ground. Damn, Shaw was a hell of shot. Reed squeezed the trigger on his carbine and watched his target fall. Then there was an explosion of movement below as the rest of the team swung into action.

They were so good. Reed felt a flash of pride. He'd been a United Coalition Navy SEAL before the alien attack, and the men and women on his SEAL team had been amazing soldiers. He'd thought they were the best.

Then he'd joined Hell Squad.

They came from a mix of backgrounds. Any surviving military members had been banded together into the squads that now fought back against the aliens occupying the ruins of Sydney, Australia—once the beautiful harbor capital of the United Coalition. The Coalition was the result of the amalgamation of countries like Australia, the United States, Canada, India and some European nations.

Now Sydney was just burned-out ruins, shattered beyond repair. He didn't know about the other capital cities around the world, but it was a safe bet they were all in the same condition. He'd been on a diving vacation in Australia when the invasion hit. He'd spent months heading south to find what was left of the human military.

Reed watched Gabe move, faster than any human should be able to. The dark, intense man was a machine. He'd already taken down two raptors and beside him, Claudia—Hell Squad's lone female soldier—jammed her carbine against a raptor's chest and opened fire.

By the time Reed slid off the roof, the fight was over. Raptor bodies sprawled on the ground. Cruz was carrying a sobbing woman over to her husband, while Claudia checked the man's injuries. All in a day's work for Hell Squad.

Reed stared up at the sky. A thunderstorm was threatening on the horizon, lightning flashing in the dark clouds. Far in the distance, he saw red lights zipping across the sky, away from them, thankfully. It was a raptor ptero ship. He swung his weapon over his shoulder. He doubted the aliens would give up easily, but neither would the humans.

Reed would fight for his freedom, for the freedom of every person sheltering in Blue Mountain Base—a military base buried deep in the Blue Mountains west of Sydney—until the day he died. He knew what it was like to have everything taken from you—even your dignity. And in the past, he'd seen fellow soldiers who'd been taken captive and suffered atrocities beyond comprehension.

No one had the fucking right to do that to anyone.

His gut tightened. He'd watched one of the best soldiers he'd had the privilege of serving with be rescued from enemy hands...only to never fully recover, living a life rushing from one bad decision to another.

Yeah, he'd fight these aliens, or die trying.

An image of huge brown eyes flickered through his head. He fought for her, too. For her to be free of the ugly memories of what the aliens had done to her.

"Aw, fuck."

Marcus' harsh exclamation made Reed glance over. His boss stood at the rear of the raptor vehicle with its back door wide open.

The squad hurried over. Reed glanced in and his jaw went tight. *Fuck.*

Humans huddled inside. Some were unconscious, sprawled on the floor. Others clung to each other, staring with wide, frightened eyes.

Jesus, some of them were just kids. Reed's hands clenched on his carbine. Fuck these alien invaders to hell.

"Get 'em out." Marcus pressed a hand to his ear. "Elle, we have human survivors. Ten of them. Send the Hawk in to pick us up."

"Roger that, Marcus."

Elle Milton's smooth voice came over the line. Their comms officer was the last member of their squad. She fed them intel, raptor numbers and saved their butts when the fighting got too hot. She'd also taken on the mammoth task of smoothing out Marcus' rough edges.

"And have Emerson and the medical team on standby when we get back to base," Marcus added.

"I will," Elle responded. "Come home in one piece."

Reed caught a slight softening in the man's scarred face. Looked like Elle was having some success. Their fearless leader was so in love with the classy, young woman. Reed felt his chest tighten. Must be nice to know you had someone waiting for you.

"Hawk's here, *amigos*," Cruz said. "Let's get these people on board."

Reed looked up. For a second, he didn't see anything, then he spotted a vague shimmer in the air—it looked like a heat mirage. The shimmer changed as the Hawk pilot turned off the quadcopter's illusion system. The dark-gray copter rapidly descended to their location, its four rotors spinning. After its skids touched dirt, the soldiers began carrying the human survivors to the Hawk.

They loaded the shell-shocked people in, setting them in the seats, securing safety harnesses over them. As Reed helped the last person out of the alien vehicle—a slim, young man—he spotted something in the back. Something blinking. With a frown, he handed the man over to Shaw and climbed into the vehicle.

On the floor at the back was a small cube the size of his palm. It was black but glowed red intermittently. It looked a lot like the data crystals he knew the raptors used to store data. But the data crystals didn't glow. He picked it up. It had some weight, but wasn't very heavy, and it wasn't hot.

"Reed? What have you got?"

Marcus stood outside, his tough form silhouetted by the sun.

Reed held up the cube. "What do you think this is?"

Marcus frowned. "Hopefully not something that explodes. Elle? Reed found some raptor tech. Sending an image through now." Marcus yanked a camera off his belt and snapped a few shots.

Reed knew the drone Elle had hovering somewhere nearby would pick up the images and relay them back to base.

A moment later, Elle made a humming noise. "The pics are coming through now. Hmm, I think we've seen something like this before. Let me just check with Noah."

Noah Kim was the comp and tech genius who ran the base's tech team. He kept the lights on and all the electronics running.

"Bring it in!" Excitement rang in Elle's voice. "It's some sort of energy source. We found one before, but it wasn't operational. Natalya wants it."

Just the mention of her name made everything in Reed come to brilliant life. Dr. Natalya Vasin. Genius energy scientist. Beautiful woman. Alien torture survivor.

"Got it, Elle." Reed slipped the energy cube into a small bag on his belt. "Tell her I'll drop it off to her at the comp lab."

Reed imagined Natalya at her desk, wearing one of those fitted skirts and prim white shirts she seemed to favor. They always made him want to mess her up a little. *Cool it, MacKinnon. She's still recovering.*

Cruz appeared. "Survivors are loaded. Let's get back to base for a cold beer and a warm woman."

Shaw snorted from near the Hawk. "Easy for you, you have a woman waiting for you. Some of us have to work to find ours."

Claudia sniffed. "And you have to work extra had to make up for your lack of personality and lack of stamina."

Shaw raised a brow. "Ha, look who's talking, Miss Snarky Sharp Edges. No one could get close enough to you without suffering cuts."

Claudia gave him an icy smile and shot him the finger before she bounded into the Hawk.

Reed climbed in, casting one last glance around the ruined suburb surrounding them. The storm was getting closer, the smell of impending rain in the air. He breathed deep and savored it. He was grateful to be at base, but he hated being hemmed in. He breathed again. He missed the ocean, and the mountains—real ones, not what passed for mountains here in very flat Australia. The underground tunnels of the base and the recycled air kept them safe and comfortable, but sometimes he felt the walls closing in on him.

And he didn't have a warm woman to snuggle up to. As the Hawk took off, he grabbed a handhold on the roof. Marcus had Elle. Cruz had the lovely and dangerous Santha. Even silent, scary Gabe had managed to hook up with the base's smart, sexy doctor. Claudia was a frequent attendee at the base's regular Friday night gatherings, but if she had a special somebody, she was keeping it quiet. Shaw was the opposite, quite happily working his way through the single ladies at base.

Reed stifled a sigh. Since the attack, most people happily embraced casual sex. It was a way to celebrate life, stay sane, and feel close to someone. But while the offers had come in regularly and frequently, Reed had deflected them with a smile and a wink. He wasn't exactly sure why. He loved women, in all their shapes and sizes. Before the attack, when he was on leave, he'd always found someone to cozy up to. Usually some athletic type who loved the outdoors, like he did. But he never let it get serious—not when he could be shipped out to God-knew-where at any minute. He'd liked his life free and unattached.

But now—he fingered the cube in his pocket— now he felt a hankering for something else.

And unfortunately the woman he wanted wasn't ready for what he had to offer.

***

Natalya Vasin stared at her comp screen scrutinizing the data displayed there. *Hmm...* As she pondered the problem, she lifted the tiny photovoltaic cell from her desk. She'd pulled it apart, working on a solution to make it more efficient. Shaped like a leaf, the cell sat on disguised trees above the base, absorbing the sunlight, and powering the secret human haven below.

Since she'd been at Blue Mountain Base, she'd extended the daily hot water availability from two hours in the morning to all through the daylight hours. But she really wanted to get hot water twenty-four hours a day. It was her own private little goal. She *loved* her showers. Even more so after she'd been unable to have one for four long, horrifying months.

As her throat closed, she swallowed and forced the memories away. *You're in Blue Mountain Base. You aren't there anymore.*

The tightness eased enough to let air into her chest.

She turned back to her comp screen, and shoved her glasses farther up on her nose. She still wasn't used to the heavier black frames, but in an apocalypse you couldn't be picky. She'd lost her lovely wire frames in the initial invasion as the alien bombs had fallen. Thankfully, she only needed to wear her glasses when her eyes were tired and strained from too much time in front of the comp screen. She jotted a few notations on her tablet and read them again. Yes, that would help, and maybe give them another two percent output. But she knew it wouldn't be enough.

Then her gaze shifted to the tiny piece of amber glass resting on the desk.

The tightness in her chest returned and she purposely slowed her breathing. The innocuous piece of glass was an alien substance. From a tank used to trap humans...and turn them into aliens.

Memories rushed at her. The sounds of the raptors, the scary sight of their strange organic technology, the scent of their lab, the horrible sounds of wailing. Her own screams. Her hand went to her neck and she felt it...the top of the ugly scar that ran down her chest.

They'd experimented on her. They'd cut and hacked into her body.

And Natalya was no longer the woman she'd been before.

Before the invasion, she'd been a renowned energy scientist, and a guest lecturer at the Sydney University. She'd been hired by energy companies to consult for exorbitant amounts of money. She'd been confident, certain of herself, normal.

Then the aliens had broken her.

No. She slammed her fist down on the desk, rattling the comp screen. She might be battered, but she wasn't broken. She'd put back on all the weight she'd lost in the raptor lab—Doc Emerson had been forcing high-calorie meal replacements into her for weeks. She was working. She was being useful.

And she was damn well going to be normal again. She was also going to do her bit to fight back against the raptors.

Her gaze fell on the amber glass once more.

Preliminary scans had shown it was an excellent semiconductor. They might be able to use it, integrate it into the base's energy system and boost the supply.

Girding herself, Natalya made herself pick the glass up.

Up close, she saw tiny black striations running through it. They were irregular and looked almost like veins.

She picked up her hand-held analyzer and ran it over the glass. She studied the results, her eyes narrowing as she pondered the implications. Maybe, just maybe, they could splice thin layers of it into the photovoltaic cells. But she needed to run a lot of tests on it first. And needed to make sure this alien tech wasn't...alive and able to do damage.

The comp lab door opened and she looked over her shoulder.

Reed. She stilled, a slight tremble running though her.

He was still wearing the bottom half of his black carbon-fiber armor, but he'd removed the chest plates, leaving him in a tight, white T-shirt that stretched over wide shoulders and left muscled, tanned arms bare. His tousled brown hair was streaked with gold. He radiated life and vitality, and the scent of him made her think of the sea.

His face was bold, with strong lines, and he had eyes the color of polished gold. A lion's eyes. That's exactly what she thought of every time she saw Reed MacKinnon—a healthy lion on the prowl for a sunny spot to lie in. Or prey to hunt.

Oh, and she'd do anything to be that prey. She was pretty sure the sexy soldier would be shocked to know the secret, X-rated fantasies she'd had about him.

"Hey, Natalya."

She managed a nod. "Reed."

"How are you doing?" he asked in his lazy drawl.

"Fine." She barely controlled the snap in her voice. He always asked her that, watching her with that patient gaze. She suspected all he saw when he looked at her was a damaged, fragile woman. He'd been the one to carry her out of that raptor lab when Hell Squad had gone in to rescue survivors. He'd been the one she'd clung to. He'd been the one to sit by her bed in the infirmary for days as she'd recovered. And he'd been the one who'd witnessed a few of her bad moments in the weeks that followed her rescue.

She wasn't damaged, dammit. She took a deep breath. "You're back from the mission?" *Oh, brilliant, Natalya, of course he was back from the mission.*

He tilted his head, watching her. "Yeah. Rescued some humans the raptors were dragging off."

To another lab, probably. Natalya swallowed the lump in her throat. But, she reminded herself Reed himself had blown up the alien's secret Genesis Facility where they'd been turning humans into aliens.

"I found this." He held up a black cube. It pulsed with a red light.

Oh. She jumped up and snatched it from him. "It's an energy source. I studied one that was damaged, but this...it looks like it's in perfect working order." She looked up and found Reed staring at her. "What?"

"Never seen you look so...covetous of anything before."

She felt heat in her cheeks. "You haven't seen me about to get in a hot shower."

Something flashed in his eyes and Natalya did a mental groan. God, had that really come out of her mouth? She'd never been this silly around a man before. She turned her back on him, knowing her cheeks were flaming now.

She set the cube on her desk and ran a hand through her short hair. Another thing she could thank the aliens for. She'd loved the long dark hair she'd once sported, but the aliens had shorn it off. At least it had grown back enough, and with a decent cut, the short style didn't look half bad.

Reed edged closer, his big body lightly brushing against hers. "So, you think the aliens use this cube as a power source? Like a battery?"

At that one tiny, accidental touch, she felt a spark of electricity skate through her. She tried to ignore his effect on her and focus on his words. "I don't know anything for certain. I need to study it more, but I'm hoping it could be an energy source we can use or..."

"Or?"

Their eyes clashed. "Something we can use against them."

His gaze sharpened. "Really?"

She shrugged a shoulder. "I don't know yet." Her jaw tightened. "But if we can, then I'll make it happen."

READY FOR ANOTHER?

ACTION
ADVENTURE
TREASURE HUNTS
SEXY SCI-FI ROMANCE

Dr. Eos Rai has spent a lifetime dedicated to her mother's dream of finding the long-lost *Mona Lisa*. When Eos uncovers tantalizing evidence of Star's End—the last known location of the masterpiece— she's shocked when her employer, the Galactic

Institute of Historic Preservation, refuses to back her expedition. Left with no choice, Eos must trust the most notorious treasure hunter in the galaxy, a man she finds infuriating, annoying and far too tempting.

Dathan Phoenix can sniff out relics at a stellar mile. With his brothers by his side, he takes the adventures that suit him and refuses to become a lazy, bitter failure like their father. When the gorgeous Eos Rai comes looking to hire him, he knows she's trouble, but he's lured into a hunt that turns into a wild and dangerous adventure. As Eos and Dathan are pushed to their limits, they discover treasure isn't the only thing they're drawn to...but how will their desire survive when Dathan demands the *Mona Lisa* as his payment?

The Phoenix Adventures

At Star's End
In the Devil's Nebula
On a Rogue Planet
Beneath a Trojan Moon
Beyond Galaxy's Edge
On a Cyborg Planet

Also by Anna Hackett

Hell Squad
Marcus
Cruz
Gabe
Reed

The Anomaly Series
Time Thief
Mind Raider
Soul Stealer
Salvation

Perma Series
Winter Fusion

The WindKeepers Series
Wind Kissed, Fire Bound
Taken by the South Wind
Tempting the West Wind
Defying the North Wind
Claiming the East Wind

Standalone Titles
Savage Dragon
Hunter's Surrender
One Night with the Wolf

Anthologies
A Galactic Holiday
Moonlight (UK only)
Vampire Hunter (UK only)
Awakening the Dragon (UK Only)

About the Author

I'm passionate about **action romance**. I love stories that combine the thrill of falling in love with the excitement of action, danger and adventure. I'm a sucker for that moment when the team is walking in slow motion, shoulder-to-shoulder heading off into battle. I write about people overcoming unbeatable odds and achieving seemingly impossible goals. I like to believe it's possible for all of us to do the same.

My books are mixture of action, adventure and sexy romance and they're recommended for anyone who enjoys fast-paced stories where the boy wins the girl at the end (or sometimes the girl wins the boy!)

For release dates, action romance info, free books, and other fun stuff, sign up for the latest news here:

Website: AnnaHackettBooks.com